She noticed the bed was large and modern

Kate caught herself on the edge of hysterical laughter. What did it matter what the bed looked like?

Frightened, she listened as Jerome matter-of-factly explained that the villa was rather primitive, but he could arrange to have water heated if she wanted to bathe.

"Oh, no!" she babbled. "A cold shower will do. I just feel so...." All at once she felt the sting of tears and a lump in her throat. "I can't," she whispered, uneasily eyeing the bed.

"Welshing on our agreement, Kate?" Jerome said unsympathetically. "You've worn that martyred look since Saturday. I haven't forced you into anything."

"Yes, you have!" she flung back. "You would have taken Philip away from me!"

"Then we'd better hope that Philip is worth the sacrifice."

Hell Is My Heaven

by

JENETH MURREY

Harlequin Books

TORONTO • LONDON • LOS ANGELES • AMSTERDAM
SYDNEY • HAMBURG • PARIS • STOCKHOLM • ATHENS • TOKYO

Original hardcover edition published in 1981
by Mills & Boon Limited

ISBN 0-373-02483-5

Harlequin edition published June 1982

CHAPTER ONE

'My daddy coming today, Auntie Kate?'

'No, not today, darling.'

'Tomorrow. Come tomorrow?'

Kate Forrest sighed as she lifted the little boy on to his chair where his short fat legs stuck out under the table. It was like having a record stuck in a groove; the same question came every day, and every day she gave the same answer.

'Could be,' she smiled at him encouragingly as she fitted the spoon into his chubby hand.

'Want my daddy!' The little mouth squared off into a mutinous line and Kate felt again the helplessness and inadequacy which these questions always brought. How did one explain to a three-year-old that he no longer had a 'Daddy'? How could she explain to him that his little world had been reduced to just three people—herself, an uncle, who at all costs must be avoided, and a grandmother, equally to be avoided! She gazed out through the small diamond-paned window at the low fuchsia hedge which bounded the small garden and at the wide stretch of Bodmin Moor which lay beyond the hedge.

This cottage would be an ideal place in the summer when the hedge blossomed and sunlight coloured the moor. Then silly things, like having no piped water supply, no drains and no proper electricity and gas supplies would be fun. She and Philip could have played out on the moor, pretending to catch butterflies and watching rabbits. They could have done a host of things, but it wasn't summer. It wasn't even spring! It would be at least two months before spring could even be expected, and the moor lay grey and grim in the early twilight, rain squalls sweeping across it as they had been sweeping across ever since she and Philip had come here four months ago.

While she filled a plastic bowl with hot water from the kettle, added soap powder to it and started washing Philip's small socks, her mind flicked back those four months and she was standing in Gerald's small flat once more. Gerald had been willing to help, but only at a price, and Kate had not been willing to pay that price.

'What you need is respectability,' he had said. 'And how much more respectable can you get than as my wife? The lawful spouse of a Fellow with the chair in Political Science at a well known and highly reputable university. Nobody would dare challenge that! And if they did, I'd give them a run for their money, the arrogant capitalists! Nobody should be allowed to be as rich as they are. They've never had to really work for anything, it's all been handed to them on a plate. Marry me, Kate, and we'll fight them together.'

'No!' Her face had whitened. 'You don't seem to understand, Gerald. I don't want to marry anybody, and in any case, you're too good a friend to be used like that. You think you're safe from them, but you're not, you'd be putting your whole career in jeopardy. The Manfreds are too powerful for you, Gerald. You've worked hard for your position and they could have it taken away from you so easily, you must know that! No, Gerald,' she shook her head decisively, 'I won't be the ruin of your career.'

They had argued about it for some time, Gerald's blue eyes glowing while his fingers worried his over-long red hair into an untidy mop on his head. The thought

crept into her mind that Gerald seemed more interested
in the political nuances than in the real issue, but she
had dismissed the thought as unworthy. Gerald was her
friend and he was offering to help in the only way he
knew, but he was no match for the Manfreds.

So she had gone to Helen. Dear Helen, her only other
friend.

'Somewhere to hide!' Helen had laughed scornfully,
not that the scorn or the laughter were in the least hurt-
ful, they came of long acquaintance and a mutual
understanding. 'Where on earth do you think you can
hide? Since that last magazine issue with your face all
over the cover and the magazine all over every bookstall
in the country, you couldn't hide in a hole in the
ground!'

'It's not as bad as that,' Kate had smiled softly. 'I
don't work under my own name, you know that, and
the pictures aren't so very much like me, the real me.
Most of it's photographic trickery. Nobody's going to
connect Kate Forrest, schoolteacher, with Noelle Lowe,
model and current sex symbol, and if I wash my face
it's even more unlikely.'

'True,' Helen had nodded sagely. 'You could go back
to Kate Forrest, schoolmarm—tweeds, thick stockings,
lace-up shoes and a felt hat, shapeless, of course.' Helen
looked at Kate with near envy. 'Be sensible, Kate.
Tweeds and a shapeless felt hat aren't going to help you
at all. You'd make them look like a million dollars and
probably start a whole new trend.' She had dragged
Kate across the room to stand in front of a full length
mirror. 'For heaven's sake,' she scolded, 'look at yourself clearly for once. You always were a stunner, and
since you took up modelling, you've learned quite a few
tricks. You'll never be able to unlearn them now—that
walk of yours, the way you hold your head. Kate, if you

think you can go back to the schoolmarm image, you're out of your tiny mind!'

Kate had looked at her own reflection and had been unconvinced. All she saw was an above average height young woman with dark chestnut hair; slender enough to be a model yet shapely so that the clothes she wore looked as if a woman was wearing them. Her face was a perfect oval, but lots of girls had oval faces, and all photographers ever wanted was that she paint and shape the features to their liking. Her eyes—she blinked them swiftly. They were a dead give-away, and she was honest enough to admit it. They seemed huge in her pale face, long and an odd clear, pale green and fringed with long silky black lashes. But eyes could be hidden, she comforted herself. Tinted glasses would do for a start.

'But I'm desperate, Helen.' She had sat down suddenly on the nearest chair. 'Honestly, love, I need help. I must hide myself and a small boy until everything's died down. I have to establish a new image or re-establish the old one. I've done it once, I can do it again.' Her mouth firmed. 'I'm not letting them have Philip. The Manfreds would corrupt him as they corrupted his father.'

Helen had gone to peer out of the window at the thickening October dusk. 'But can't you do it legally? I'd have thought that an aunt had just as much right to bring up a nephew as an uncle.'

Kate's laugh had been grimly bitter. 'Everything being equal, yes! But everything's not equal, is it? Perhaps, if I'd stayed a schoolteacher, I'd have stood a better chance, but not now. Not when I'm what I am and the uncle's a millionaire and the grandmother hobnobs with the upper crust—and don't try to tell me that money and social standing don't matter. They do, and you know it, that's why I've come to you.'

'You aren't without the odd bob or two yourself.' Helen hadn't been being difficult, she had been being practical and getting things straight in her mind.

'But where did I get my "odd bob or two"? Modelling!' Kate had grimaced fastidiously. 'Make-up, hair-styles, clothes—remember the clothes, Helen? Cleavages to the waist and skirts slit beyond what's decent. Negligees which left absolutely nothing to the imagination, bikinis made of a couple of daisies and a fig leaf, and everything recorded for posterity in colour or glossy finished black and white. What court in the country would choose me when Philip's grandmother sits in a stately home with servants who call her 'madam' and his uncle conducts his amorous affairs discreetly on a private yacht? What chance has a twenty-six-year-old teacher turned model against that? Even if they couldn't find anything else wrong with me, they would point out that I'd have to work to keep him so I couldn't give him all my time.'

'Mmm, I see your point,' Helen had frowned. 'From where I'm standing, it looks as though you're a bit short on trumps.'

'I've none at all!' Kate laughed wryly.

'Then you'd better have the cottage,' Helen had grinned impishly. 'Nobody's going to look for "Noelle Lowe" in a lonely cottage on Bodmin Moor, especially at this time of year. Late October isn't the time for the Moor. All the home comforts, of a sort,' she had continued. 'Cylinders of Calor gas for a small cooker and a fridge, water from a well in the garden, but you don't have to fetch water in a bucket, there's a small rotary pump in the kitchen and you pump it up to a tank in the roof. You pump to fill the tank every night. There aren't any drains either, but the septic tank is very efficient. How will that do you?'

Kate sighed with relief. 'Give me the key and a few

directions—it sounds ideal. We'll leave right after the funeral, Philip and I. I want to be away from London as soon as possible, so I'll give you a cheque for six months' rent, and if anybody comes asking questions. . . .'

'I don't know nuthin'!' Helen had grinned. 'Only two more questions, though. Who is going to the funeral, Kate Forrest or Noelle Lowe, and why do you think there'll be a hue and cry?'

'Noelle will be attending the funeral.' Kate looked bitter. 'It's expected of her. "Noelle Lowe, the glamorous model and sister to the late Mrs Theo Manfred, attending the funeral of her sister, who with her brother-in-law was killed in a car crash a week ago". Noelle will be there in haute couture black, and that will be her last ever performance. As for why I think they'll be looking for me, or rather Noelle—they'll want Philip! Nobody's said anything, but I just know.'

It had been raining and underfoot the cemetery was soggy. Miss Noelle Lowe watched from the shelter of a distant tree, a tall, slim, veiled figure in black. She had been glad of the veil because behind it she could let her tears run unchecked. The heap of raw earth looked obscene—so much earth taken out for Shirley's small body. She had closed her eyes and Shirley had sprung to life behind her lids, blonde and with a chocolate-box prettiness, small and fluffy like a cream Persian kitten. She had been so happy with her perpetual train of admirers and happy with her young, wealthy husband until the gilt had worn off Theo's gingerbread. Shirley had blamed her pregnancy for that. How, she had asked, could Theo find her attractive when she looked like a whale? But it would be all right when the baby was born. Theo would come back to her.

More tears pricked under Kate's eyelids and she had squeezed this new flood back, but why shouldn't she cry? Shirley had been a loved little sister, a stepsister but no less loved for that, and the fact that she had married a child of a man couldn't alter it. A spoiled, vicious child of a man who had abandoned Shirley when she had needed him most and had then come back to her when it suited him. A child who wanted anything that was out of reach and who had been blessed or cursed with sufficient money to buy anything and anybody he fancied.

Kate had watched the group at the graveside, too far away for them to see her properly, and she was devoutly thankful for that. She hadn't gone into the small chapel to hear the service, she had waited in the shelter of her tree and watched the Manfred family come out, and the sight of them had given her goose pimples. Mrs Manfred, a statuesque, silvery blonde, had not looked a comfortable sort of person, and Theo's elder brother didn't look comfortable either. She received a vivid impression of a dark, implacable ruthlessness, and she decided he had a lean and hungry look. The schoolteacher in her remembered her Shakespeare, 'such men are dangerous'. Several times during the ceremony at the graveside, she had seen his black head turn in her direction and she had crept back farther behind her tree. She didn't want to meet him or his mother; they were both strangers to her because when Shirley had married Theo Manfred it had been a whirlwind affair and Kate had been escorting a group of schoolchildren on a tour of Paris. When Kate had returned, Shirley had been away on honeymoon in Crete and after that she had moved into a lush apartment, so that Kate had rarely seen her.

Visits from Shirley had been few and far between and

the Manfreds had been far too haughty to bring themselves down to the level of an ordinary schoolteacher
who was, after all, only a stepsister. That was the way
she had worked it out in her mind.

She remembered Shirley's agonised little face when
she had come visiting before the baby was born.

'He doesn't even look at me any more. He hasn't ever
since I started on the baby,' Shirley had wailed the words
through a flood of tears.

'Leave him!' Kate had been unsympathetic.

'No! Why should I?' There had been a mulish look
about Shirley's pink and white prettiness. 'I'm to be the
mother of his child and I love him.' But a few weeks
later she had left him, coming to Kate in the evening
with a taxi full of luggage, none of which was suitable
for a mother-to-be. 'I won't go back,' she had stormed.
'Theo's gone off to Italy, he says it's business and he
refused to take me with him. He said it was because of
the baby coming, but I know better. They all treat me
like dirt. Theo uses me as if I was somebody he'd
bought, and when I complained, he offered to pay me!'
Her voice had risen in shrill outrage. 'And his mother
laughs at me,' she had muttered, and Kate had suddenly
found herself with two people to keep on her salary.
Gerald had been a tower of strength at that time. It was
he who had found her extra work, teaching commercial
English to evening classes in the local technical college,
and for a while they had managed very well. But then
the baby was born and after that Kate learned a lot of
new things, like babies grow at an alarming rate and
clothes which fit today will be too small next week—
and of course, Shirley's life of luxury had spoiled her
for the little economies of life.

Kate had suggested asking the Manfreds for help, but
Shirley had been violently opposed to it.

'They don't want me, but they'd take Philip, if they could get him. As it is now, they don't know where I am and I'm not going to tell them, not yet. If they want my baby, they'll have to take me with him.'

'But surely,' Kate had been confused, 'they know you're here with me? Where else could you be?'

Shirley had flushed. 'They don't know about you,' she had been reluctant to admit it. 'Oh, don't look like that, as if I'd done something dreadful. It all started out as a joke, Theo was—er—interested in me and I played Little Orphan Annie, all alone in the big, cruel world. He went all protective about me, then after we were together, I couldn't spring you on him, not after more than a year, could I?'

Kate had closed her mouth firmly until her pity for Shirley had overwhelmed her momentary anger. Shirley had not seemed to notice, her mind was too busy with another facet of the problem of how to keep three people on a salary designed for one.

'What about that photographer you met?' she had enquired. 'Didn't he offer you a job modelling? Why don't you take that? You'd earn far more than you do with your silly old schoolteaching.'

And so 'Noelle Lowe' was born; successfully after the first bad start—but Kate preferred to forget that bad start. It had been something she wasn't particularly proud of, an embarrassing humiliation and a complete waste of time. But the whole thing had been a waste of time, not just the first part, because within six months, when Philip was nearly a year old, Shirley was back with her young husband and a life full of sweetness and light, and Kate was stuck with 'Noelle Lowe'.

She remembered Shirley's glowing face, just a week ago when she had tumbled through the door of Kate's flat with Philip, now a sturdy three-year-old. 'A second honeymoon!' Shirley had been so happy. 'Isn't it crazy after all this time? But we can't go on a honeymoon with a three-year-old kid, can we? It would spoil it all completely. There just wouldn't be an ounce of romance in it. Look after him for me, Kate. I've told Theo about you and he's quite agreeable. See you when we get back,' and she had whirled away to Theo and the car crash.

Kate came back to the present, to the tiny, stone-flagged kitchen, the rough plastered walls washed white, the low, raftered ceiling and the red and white checked curtains at the small window. While her thoughts had been wandering, Philip had engaged in a game with the puppy she had bought him, a game involving pellets of bread which the pup was supposed to catch and eat. Kate smiled at them as she rinsed out the socks. What were a few bread pellets on the floor?

Wrinkling her nose at the primitive conditions—she still wasn't used to them after nearly four months—she went to fetch the small galvanised bath from the back shed, bringing it to the rug in front of the kitchen fire. There was cold water all ready in a large enamel jug and the black iron kettle on the trivet of the grate was puffing steam from its spout.

'Bath time, Philip,' she called, and watched his young face grow mutinous.

'Want to play.' The boy turned back to the dog. 'Want Daddy,' she heard him mutter.

She ignored his wilfulness. It had been an upsetting time for him. He had been deprived of both father and mother and his whole life had changed overnight. He was such a little boy and he was bound to feel unsure of himself and everybody. Kate wondered vaguely why his perpetual call was for his father, he never asked for 'Mummy'—but then, she argued, Philip would have seen his mother frequently during the day and his father less often. Perhaps Theo was looked on as a bringer of gifts, sweets and suchlike. But it was one of those little problems which would never be solved. Philip was the only one who could tell her and he was incapable of doing that.

Kate returned to present problems. She and Philip had been in this cottage for months, months of wintry weather with almost incessant rain from drizzling grey skies which made any outdoor activities almost impossible. There had been some clear, cold days, but they had been very few, and even Christmas had been a disappointment. Philip had wished for his 'Daddy' and with the best will in the world, that was one wish which Kate could not grant. She had provided all the usual things, a tree with glass baubles and tinsel, to hold the brightly coloured packages, balloons and streamers, cake, mince pies and a pudding, but the two cards on the mantelpiece, one from her to Philip and one from Helen, had looked lonely. A spartan Christmas, but that was how it had to be. While there were just the two cards, she was safe.

She arranged the minute striped pyjamas on a chair by the fire to warm and made splashing noises with the bathwater. Philip came at once then, eager to join in this new game. He was squealing with laughter and splashing suds at her, defying her order to come out, when a deep voice spoke from the kitchen door.

'Having trouble, Miss Lowe?'

Both Kate and Philip turned to the door; Kate did it while an icy band tightened round her heart, but Philip took one look, screamed 'Daddy!' with obvious joy and wriggling out of the bath, flung his wet, soapy body at the man leaning negligently against the doorpost. Philip was fended off as the man crossed the room and took the towel from Kate's nerveless fingers to wrap around the child.

'He calls everybody "Daddy",' Kate heard her own
voice with surprise. It was saying the wrong thing. She
should have been up in arms at this intrusion by a
stranger and she knew she should have said so, but this
wasn't a stranger, not to her. And she had been fearing
this for four long months. But she couldn't say any
more, her voice was going to wobble and he would
know! She sat back on her heels and schooled her face
to a quiet mask as she looked up at him. He was now
wielding the towel in a competent way.

'Especially when the resemblance is so marked.' He
was rubbing the boy dry.

Kate rose, folded her mouth tightly and set about
outstaring the intruder. Now that the initial shock was
over, some of her courage was returning. While she was
doing this, she was assessing him. The resemblance was
there, but it wasn't that marked. Perhaps the hair
was the same, black, thick and wavy, but the intruder's
was silvering at the temples while Theo's had been a
youthful jet. Maybe, if Theo had grown older, his face
would have thinned down to these harsh, arrogant
planes. Yes, this was what Theo would have looked like
in ten years' time if he had learned discipline and self-
control. Then his weak, rather greedy mouth would have
looked like the intruder's long curve of thin lips and
Theo's eyes might have had the same world-weary droop
of heavy lids. With an effort, Kate pulled herself together. This man frightened her, and she searched for
some sign of weakness in the dark, harsh face, but there
was none. He had frightened her at the funeral, but to
show that fear would mean that her battle was lost
before it had begun. Kate mentally fired her first shot.

'Do you make a habit of walking into strange houses
without knocking?' Frost was thick on her tongue.

'But if I had knocked, would you have answered the door, Miss Lowe?' One black eyebrow was raised as he set about inserting Philip into his pyjamas.

Kate lifted her chin. 'There's some mistake,' she said coolly, and hoped that her inward trembling didn't show. 'I don't know who has misdirected you, but you've come to the wrong house. Who were you looking for?' Her expression was now one of polite enquiry with a shred of distaste for the uninvited.

'I was looking for you.' He fastened the button on the waistband of the pyjama bottoms and started to insert Philip's stout little torso into the top half.

Kate automatically became the schoolteacher. 'Wrong house,' she said briskly and without regret. 'I'm afraid I can't be of much help, we're strangers here, but if you go down to the village, it's only about four miles. . . .'

The firelight shone on the planes of his face, giving them a carved look as if they had been chiselled out of some dark stone. He was expressionless. 'No, not the wrong house, Miss Noelle Lowe!' It wasn't a question, it was a statement, and the chill of fear crept closer to her heart.

'Forrest,' she corrected with a polite, meaningless smile. 'Katherine Forrest.'

He smiled at her pityingly. 'Ah yes, Kate Forrest, little Shirley's stepsister who was born on Christmas Day and whose mother's maiden named was Lowe—and this,' he touched the boy's curly head, 'this is my nephew, Philip. Do correct me if I'm wrong.'

Suddenly Kate's legs began to tremble. She had been fearing this for so long, it seemed like for ever. It had been a nightmare, both waking and sleeping, ever since Shirley had been killed, and now it had happened as she had known it would and all her machinations had been to no avail. A dark whirlpool was closing over her head, shutting out the warm kitchen and engulfing her in a chilly flood. She felt herself pushed into a chair and as if from a great distance, she heard his voice.

'Where does the boy sleep?'

'Upstairs,' she mumbled through stiff lips. 'On the right.'

He moved quietly for such a big man. She hardly heard his footstep on the steep, narrow staircase, either going up or coming down again. There was little sound either as he went along the stone-flagged passage to the front door. She felt a chill draught as he opened it, heard the click of the garden gate and the solid 'thunk' of an expensive car door closing. Then the draught stopped and he was back in the kitchen once more.

'Drink this,' and she opened her eyes to a glass half full of golden liquid. Distaste wrinkled her nose at the fumes of brandy.

'I don't drink.' With a cold hand she pushed the glass away.

'Drink it!' He hadn't raised his voice and she watched the long-fingered brown hand bring the glass back and raise it so that she felt the cold rim pressing against her mouth. 'Drink.' It was a soft command. The pressure on her mouth grew greater, bruising her lip, and because there was nothing else she could do, she drank.

'Better now?'

Kate felt the brandy running warm down into her stomach and some of the cold fear withdrew into a cold knot in her chest.

'Tea now, I think.' He sounded quite casual as he moved about the kitchen, fetching milk from the small gas fridge, cups and saucers from the dresser and lighting the jets under the kettle on the Calor gas stove. When the tea came, it was hot, sweet and strong; reviving her so that life stirred once more in her frozen body.

She had lost her battle, she knew that without being told. Had she sensed any weakness in this man, she would have fought and felt that there was some point to it, there would have been a chance of her winning, but there was no weakness. Nonetheless, she had to try.

'He's my sister's child. You can't have him.' She raised defiant eyes. 'Shirley asked me to look after him, not you, not your mother. Me!'

He sat down opposite her, arranging his long legs under the table and leaning back in his chair. His eyes held hers with a brooding look.

'Money talks, Kate. We want the boy.'

'Don't call me Kate,' she snapped, some small courage returning. 'I don't allow that familiarity from strangers, and you are a stranger. I don't even know your name,' she muttered the last inconsequentially. 'Shirley always called you "Jo". As for money talking, that's what I'd have expected from you and your mother. You think you can buy anything.'

'We can.' He was tranquil. 'If it was necessary, we could buy evidence, irrefutable evidence that Noelle Lowe is not a fit person to have the care of a child. But it isn't necessary. I already have the evidence, we don't have to buy more.'

Kate clenched her fingers about the cup and her face whitened. 'Filth!' She hissed the word at him.

'You took your clothes off,' he pointed out calmly.

'No. I didn't, not completely.' A light of battle was dawning in her eyes and her fear was relegated to the background. 'It was what's known as 'artistic calendar work' and I was decently if briefly clothed.'

'Titillating is a better description. Did you ever wonder what happened to those pictures, Kate?'

'No,' she glared at him. 'I'd been paid and I didn't care any more. I was just thankful. . . . And you know why I did it!' Despair made her defiant. 'Shirley wanted out. She came to me and begged. For a while, we managed, but it all got too expensive and I had to find money somehow. Your precious brother treated her like a—a thing! He used to offer to pay her! He used her, and your mother laughed!' She shuddered, even now the thought made her sick. 'Shirley asked me for help and I did what I had to do and I'm glad! Glad!' she repeated. 'You're filth, the three of you—you, your brother and your mother. Now, get out! Get out of my house, Mr Manfred, and don't come back.'

'The name is Jerome.' He remained calm and relaxed as if he hadn't heard her tirade. 'The photographs—I had them suppressed, but I still have the negatives, and this is not your house. It belongs to your friend Helen, the struggling artist. I hear her last exhibition didn't go too well. Do you think she would refuse a reasonable offer for the property? I could make it a very good offer, if I was driven to it—too good to be refused. As for Shirley, could it have really been as bad as she led you to suppose? She married Theo, didn't she? And after the boy was born, she went back to him. Or was the lure of money too strong for your empty-headed little sister?'

Kate sighed and put her head down while she re-mustered her forces. 'My sister is dead,' she spat at him, 'and empty-headed or not, I loved her. I don't think there can be much love in your family, Mr Manfred, so you wouldn't understand. As for my friend Helen, she's been a good friend, but she has to live the same as everybody else. You wouldn't know about that either, you've never had to bother about the pennies. Yes, Helen's an artist, and if her pictures don't sell, she has to look around for some other way to keep herself and buy materials for her next pictures so she can try to sell those. If she sold you this cottage, I wouldn't blame her

a bit nor think any worse of her for doing so.' She
looked up at him wearily. 'Oh, it's useless trying to explain to you. You haven't been there, you just don't
know! You sit in your superior seat and pull strings so
that poor fools like me jump about like puppets because
we did what we had to do, whether we liked it or not.'
Futile, silly tears sprang to her eyes and slowly trickled
down her cheeks. 'I'll still fight,' she whispered huskily.

'With what?' Calmly he produced cigarettes and a
lighter. 'You have nothing to fight with, Kate, not one
single weapon—and besides, you've forgotten something.' He sounded almost amused. 'You've flung a
great number of insults about, you've insulted my
mother, you've insulted my brother, who can no longer
defend himself, and you've insulted me. This is a lonely
cottage and I could exact payment for those insults, a
very pleasant payment, and who would believe you if
you said I forced you?'

'And will you leave money on the table as your
brother did to my sister?' Kate's voice was hoarse with
bitterness.

'There may be no need if you're reasonable.'

'Oh, I'm reasonable,' she looked hate at him. 'I know
when I'm beaten.'

'Good! That, then, is the end of the preliminaries.
We can now get down to some serious business.'
Thoughtfully, he studied the burning end of his cigarette
and pushed the case and the lighter across to her. 'I
prefer to bargain from a position of strength, and in
this case my position is so strong that I don't have to
bargain at all.'

She pushed the case and lighter back across the table
to him with a slight shake of her head. 'I don't smoke.'

'No vices?'

Kate ignored the question.

'No, as you say, you don't have to bargain with me, you've just proved that!' She felt unutterably weary and went slack in her chair, drained of everything but the deep abiding hate which had kept her going for so long. 'Whatever you have in mind, it won't be a bargain, it'll be an ultimatum.'

'Have you any food in the house, Kate?'

She looked at him in surprise, watching as his long fingers extinguished the cigarette efficiently. There seemed to be a calm content about his mouth. His next words surprised her even more.

'I think you've been living in fear ever since your sister died, and it was all unnecessary, you know. I saw you at the funeral and I would have spoken to you then, but you slipped away like a black ghost. One minute you were there under the tree and the next, you'd gone. It would have been better if you'd waited. You could have saved yourself all these months of flight and fear. You had reason to fear,' he admitted. 'You knew I would find you. Now the fear is over and you're tired. You need food and so do I—there's a lot of me to maintain, as you can see. I suggest we eat and have a civilised conversation.'

'Civilised!' Kate looked at him wearily. 'I suppose by that you mean that you'll converse and all I'll have to do will be to say 'Yes' and 'No' in the correct places. Please go. I've got some soup and cheese and things which will do for me, you can get a meal in the village. I'll still be here when you come tomorrow. Where could I run?'

Slowly he shook his head, his expression enigmatic. 'I'm sorry, but I don't trust you, Kate. As soon as my back was turned you'd be off. I have a sixth sense about people and it's telling me that you've given in a little too easily. You have a car here somewhere and even if I immobilised it, you would walk, and carry the boy, if you had to. Any woman who would do what you did for your sister is a worthy opponent, and I treat worthy opponents with caution. No, Kate, I'll share your soup and cheese and things, and then we'll talk.'

'I'm too tired to talk.'

'Nervous reaction.' Jerome Manfred sounded practical and implacable. 'Where's the soup?'

CHAPTER TWO

DINNER, such as it was was over. Kate had apologised sarcastically for the lack of caviare, porterhouse steak and asparagus tips, her tone biting and her air one of disdain. Jerome Manfred had spared her one cool glance.

'I don't care for caviare and I consider the omelette I made to be the equal of any steak,' he observed flatteningly.

Now Kate moved about the kitchen, rinsing down the draining board, restoring crockery to the dresser and aware all the time of the big man seated comfortably by the fire, the smoke from his cigarette drifting up to the low rafters. Although he never looked her way, she was aware all the time of being watched. At the cutlery drawer she hesitated, her fingers closing round the wooden handle of the big carving knife. It fitted snugly into her palm and there was a comfortable and comforting feel about it, but it was too big for concealment. And where would it get her? she thought drearily. Only as far as the nearest gaol, and then Philip would go to his grandmother for certain. Besides, she wasn't at all sure that she could do it. It would take a peculiar kind of courage or madness to stick a knife in somebody, and she didn't think she had that sort of courage—and despite her months of hiding and worry, she wasn't mad. Reluctantly she let her fingers slide from the smooth, well shaped wood.

'You couldn't do it.'

Kate gasped and turned round swiftly. How could he know what she had been thinking?

'Don't be too sure.' Food and a quiet half hour had restored some of her natural optimism and she spoke belligerently. 'I did something once before, remember? I didn't think I could do that either, but I did!'

'But there was no blood.' He was still calm. 'You don't like blood, Kate. You faint.' He seemed filled with a cold sort of humour. 'I know every little thing about you. Now, stop fiddling and sit down. It's time we had our talk.'

She sat down quietly, but her eyes flamed as she looked at him across the table and her voice dripped acid with every word. 'You know. Of course you know! You've had your grubby little men investigating me. Pawing through my life with their dirty, curious fingers. Ugh!'

There was a wry look about his mouth. 'Shall I tell you, Kate? Yes, I think I will. You were a bonus and one I didn't expect, but it often happens that way. I started out investigating your stepsister.'

'You were investigating Shirley?' Kate allowed the disgust she felt to become evident in her voice. 'What was the matter? Didn't you trust her either?'

'Not completely.' He was calm and factual. 'I never did. Your little sister was an accomplished liar. After she went back to Theo, when Philip was nearly a year old, I trusted her even less. Too many of her stories were thin and they didn't add up. According to her she was alone in the world and, to be blunt, I suspected that there was another man. I'm a business man, Kate, and I can't afford to take chances, so your little sister was investigated. And what did I find? I found Miss Katherine Forrest, a stepsister, but even so nobody of whom Shirley should have been ashamed. It puzzled me, and yet at the same time it explained several mysteries. It explained how Shirley could vanish from the face of the earth for more than a year, how she could live without working, how she could have a baby without any money or without drawing any state benefits and afterwards live with the baby without having to consider adoption or having to work for a living. And when she was reunited with Theo, she chattered like a whole group of parakeets and yet not one word of Kate Forrest. Never, either before her marriage or afterwards, did she mention you.'

Kate shrugged. 'Why should she? We were only step-sisters, we weren't so close.'

'Lies, Kate!' He sounded tired. 'I'm weary of lies. Shirley was living with you when she ran away with Theo. You brought her up when her mother died. I know where you were born, what schools you went to. I have copies of your school reports and copies of your tutor's comments on your work at university. I have also a letter of reference from the headmistress of the school where you taught. I phoned the lady and implied that you were considering working for me and she wrote back in glowing terms, saying how much she'd missed you and what a loss your departure had been to the teaching profession.'

Kate managed an indifferent shrug. 'So?' Her voice was acid as she glared at him. 'You said we were going to talk,' she reminded him. 'What's there to talk about? We both want the same thing—Philip! Only you have all the weapons, all the heavy artillery. You can stand up in court and make me out to be just what you choose—a nude model, even though you know I was no such thing. I can't fight that! I could point out that you're a lascivious womaniser, but where would that get me? You're a man, and for some silly reason that seems to make a difference.' Angrily she sprang to her feet and stood looking down at him.

'I said we would talk, Kate. But you don't talk, you hurl insults.'

Her voice became quiet and deadly. 'I couldn't insult you, Mr Manfred. It's an impossibility to be rudely discourteous to somebody like you.'

Jerome Manfred's face became bleak and his nostrils thinned. 'Sit down! First of all we'll talk about Gerald Twyford.'

Kate sat. 'What about Gerald?' She was seething. That he should talk about insults after having her investigated like a common criminal!

'Are you his mistress?'

Kate's face flamed and then went quite white as she struggled to hold her temper. She even indulged in a little black humour.

'Don't you know? Haven't your spies been peeping in the right bedroom windows? I thought you said you knew everything, surely you've gone into that! Your spies could have reported to you where intercourse took place, how many times and the duration, I should have thought! Think of the extra weight you could use to prove that I'm not fit to have control of a child! A nude model and now a tramp!' Her voice thinned so that the next words were a hiss of hate. 'You could even buy a few other men to say I've slept with them as well. After all, there's safety in numbers, and think what it would do for you in court. You'd look ten feet tall!'

His hand came across the table to grasp hers cruelly. She looked down at it. Had she been able, she would have flung it off and gone and washed her wrist with disinfectant, but the grip was too strong. She considered the hand idly. A nice hand, long and slim, with thin brown fingers and smooth, well kept nails. She thought of Gerald's hands and shivered. Hands were a fetish with her. Gerald had thick white fingers and spatulate nails, and sometimes he bit those nails. And there were rough, red hairs on the backs of his hands and fingers. She knew that she could never have borne for those hands to touch her, not even though he had offered to help. The price of that help would have been those hands wandering over her body. She shuddered, coming back to the present and sitting erect in her chair.

Jerome Manfred's voice was nasty. 'You're wasting words and the bitterness is running out of your mouth. You need have said none of those things, all that was needed was "Yes" or "No". I would have believed you.'

'You would have believed me!' She made it sound like the eighth wonder of the world. 'My, Mr Manfred, you are trusting!'

'Very well, so you weren't his mistress. He wanted to marry you?' He rapped out the question and without thinking, she nodded. 'And you refused?' Again she nodded, and he released her wrist and sat back in his chair, apparently satisfied.

'And again you believe me?' She made her eyes round in pretended wonder while she strove for a calm to match his own. 'Mr Manfred, I don't care whether you believe me or not. I don't care anything about you. I hate you. I hate your family and I hated your brother even more. The only good thing to come out of the mess you and your family have made of Shirley's life is Philip, and you shan't spoil him, I won't let you. Somehow I'll stop you—I don't know how, but I will, if I have to get down in the slime you crawl in and fight you there!'

'Good!' He sounded pleased and his eyes gleamed with gratification. 'I'm offering you that opportunity. You may come and share our—er—slime, as you call it.' Her gasp of surprise was stifled as he raised a hand and her words hung, unspoken on her lips. 'You can hardly refuse,' he drawled aggravatingly. 'You say that you wish to care for Philip—well, you may, but only on my terms.'

'*Your* mistress?' she shook her head violently. 'No, thank you, Mr Manfred. I'm not that much of a fool. I know how long I'd last in that position—a few days at the most and then you and Philip would disappear, and what chance would I have of getting him back after that? At present, my chances of keeping him are small, but the chance is always there that you mightn't be believed by everybody when you start flinging your dirt about. But after a period, no matter how short, as your mistress, I wouldn't expect anybody to believe me.' She sat back in her chair, outwardly composed, but her eyes were wary.

He looked at her with a cynical humour. 'How you do run on, Kate! I make half a suggestion, you give me no time to complete it and you're wading in, hackles erect and willing to credit me with every vile motive your little mind can conjure up. My mistresses have invariably been willing. I've never found any need to blackmail any of them into taking the position. In any case, I haven't offered you that place in my life.'

'A sort of nanny, perhaps?' She matched his cynicism. 'With a few fringe benefits for you, of course.'

'My wife,' he corrected, and Kate looked at him, numbed with shock. She was aware of a roaring in her ears and his voice seemed to be coming from the end of a long, black tunnel so that it echoed in her head. The rest of what he said escaped her, although she thought she heard him say that he thought they would make a good partnership. It was such a ludicrous thought that she started to giggle hysterically, and then there was a blissful, quiet blackness and she sank into it with a feeling of relief.

She opened her eyes to the soft light of the oil lamp in her bedroom. She felt the softness of the pillow under her cheek and the fresh sweetness of the damp, night air on her face. She lay quietly for a few moments watching the steady yellow flame in the lamp and the memory swept back, jerking her upright convulsively. He had gone! He had taken advantage of her moment's weakness and he would be gone, and Philip with him. Fear swept through her, whitening her face, widening her eyes and making her gasp as if she had been running too fast and too far.

A hand found her shoulder and pushed her back on to the pillows. Once more, it seemed, he read her mind. 'I'm still here, and the boy is asleep in his own bed. You should try to sleep now. Tomorrow we leave for London and the journey will be long and wearying for a small child.' He rose and went to the door where a loose floorboard creaked under his foot. 'You even have an alarm!' He turned back to her with a smile which did nothing to soften his harsh features. 'Would you like me to bring you the carving knife? You have no need of it, I assure you. Not that you ever seem to fear for yourself, always it's the boy, and before him, it was your sister. Take off your clothes and rest. I'll wake you in the morning, we have to make an early start.'

'I want a drink,' Kate muttered defiantly, and swung herself off the bed, aware of her rumpled appearance. She smoothed down her skirt and buttoned up the green silk shirt she was wearing before she paddled around with her feet to find her slippers. 'I'm going to make a pot of tea.' She passed him in the doorway and stopped suddenly. 'Where do you propose sleeping?'

Jerome shrugged. 'I'll find somewhere.' He turned to follow her downstairs. 'Is there a couch in the other room?'

'Why don't you go down to the pub in the village?' She pushed open the kitchen door and was grateful for the warmth. 'They do a decent meal there and you'd get a bed easily. They don't have many visitors at this time of the year.' She was talking too much and she knew it, but somehow she couldn't stop chattering about trivialities. 'The parlour's damp, we haven't used it since we came and I haven't bothered to keep a fire in there.'

'Must I say it again, Kate?' The note of weary insolence was back in his voice. 'I don't trust you. I'm staying here!'

'Oh, you can trust me,' she flung over her shoulder to him as she reached for the kettle. 'I have to consider your offer, don't I? Who knows, it might be too good for me to refuse.'

She filled the small, light kettle from the black one on the hob and lit the burner of the gas stove and turned to find him watching her from the doorway. 'If I accept, I get what I want, which is to keep Philip,' she explained gravely. 'If I ran off with him tonight, where would it get me? Another month, perhaps, and then you'd catch up with me again. Why can't you leave us alone?' Her voice was desperate. 'Why must you have everything? Why do you want Philip? He's nothing to you. If I could only think straight, I'd probably be asking 'Why marry me at all?' You despise me and you know that you can buy Philip's custody any time you want, and you've enough money to employ a regiment of nannies.'

'With a little tuition you'll make an admirable and much admired wife.' His glance flicked over her, and under the insolent regard she lost her temper.

'Is the Butterfly Circuit beginning to pall?' She was scathing. 'Are you weary of flitting from flower to flower, or have you gone through the pack and want something different? You can marry anybody you

choose, they'll all lie down and wriggle with pleasure at
the idea. Why pick on me?'

'Philip is used to you.' Only a slight flush on his
cheekbones betrayed his anger, that and the glitter in
his eyes. 'He's lost his parents, that surely is enough for
one small boy. Then again, there's another point I'd
like to make. At present, Philip is my heir, but I want
my own children, and I want them before Philip gets
much older. I want Philip to grow up knowing that he's
not in first place—that way, he won't be disappointed—
and finally, I want an obedient wife.' He smiled nastily.
'You will be obedient, Kate, I can control you. You'd
do just as I say because, if you didn't, you'd never see
Philip again. I'm giving you no choice, am I? You want
to bring Philip up and I've shown you how you can do
it . . .'

'On your terms . . .' Kate fought back her tears.

'Certainly on my terms. You're in no position to dic-
tate terms. All you have to do is accept the inevitable.'

'Accept your offer of marriage,' she corrected him as
she moved about the kitchen, collecting the milk jug
and the sugar basin and setting them down on the table
together with a clean cup and saucer. As she did so, she
looked a question at him and when he nodded, she
added another cup and saucer. 'And of course, there's
all your lovely money.' She poured boiling water on the
tea-leaves. 'I'd be a fool to ignore that aspect, wouldn't
I? Or are you one of those millionaires who practises
strict economy and expects his wife to wear the same
hat for three years running?'

'You will receive a dress allowance which I'm sure
you'll find adequate.' The words were flat and she
suffered a disappointment at her failure to make him
lose his temper. It was so much easier to be filthy rude
to somebody who was being filthy rude to her, but he

wasn't. He was just sitting, waiting for his cup of tea and looking quite unmoved. And she wanted him to be beastly, otherwise her better nature was going to make her do something she didn't want to do. She tried again. 'If I married you, how many mistresses should I be expected to share you with?'

Jerome looked up at her thoughtfully. 'Kate, I suspect you're trying to make me lose my temper. I wonder why.'

She gave up and a spark of humour, long suppressed, glinted in her eyes. 'If you'll kindly continue to insult me as you've done since you arrived here, I shall have no compunction in bedding you down on a damp couch in a cold, damp room.'

'And the alternative?'

'You can have my bed,' she said grudgingly. 'There's a child's bed in Philip's room. It's too small for you, but I can manage there for the night. But please go on insulting me. I *want* you to be uncomfortable! I *want* you to catch pneumonia! I can think of nothing which would please me more! I've asked you to go and you've refused. I can't make you go, I'm not physically capable of throwing you out, but I warn you. . . .'

'You warn me?' His nostrils thinned. 'My good girl. . . .'

'I'm not your good girl!' she flared at his insolent condescension.

'The question is, were you ever anybody's *good* girl? Your meteoric rise to fame as a top model. . . .'

'That does it!' Kate slammed her cup down with such force that she cracked the saucer. 'Now you can damned well sleep on the couch, and I hope you catch pneumonia!'

His hand came down hard on her wrist as she made to rise from the chair, the fingers tightening on the fragile bones under the skin. 'Before you go, we'll have an agreement. A firm agreement. You will be an obedient and loving wife or. . . .'

'All right,' she said reluctantly, 'I agree to your terms, I accept—but don't think I'm looking forward to it or think that you're doing me a terrific favour. As far as I'm concerned, I can't think of anything more degrading, but if it will enable me to keep Philip, I'll grit my teeth and go through with it.'

'Then we'll seal the bargain.' He jerked swiftly at her wrist, bringing her against him in a stumbling run and his free hand fastened in the thick pleat of hair at the back of her head, holding and pulling so that her face was tilted to his.

Kate kept her eyes open; it was a trick she had discovered and it usually worked. Men, for some reason, didn't relish kissing women who kept their eyes open. But this time the trick didn't work. Jerome's mouth took hers in open insult so that she wanted to scream, and he took his time about it, demanding a response until she was too exhausted to fight any longer and she softened against him and her eyes drifted shut.

When he at last raised his head, there were tears trickling down her face, tears of fright and some other emotion which was new to her and which she couldn't name, but she tilted her chin bravely.

'Is that how it's going to be?' she whispered the question. 'Because, if it is, I think I'd rather die.'

'Than give me Philip.' He was emotionless.

'No!' Her eyes were still glittering with tears. 'I'll marry you. You said you needed a wife—well, you've got one, but you'll regret it, Mr Manfred, I'll make sure of that!' And she fled up the stairs to seek safety in Philip's bedroom.

Kate did not sleep well. The child's bed was narrow

and hard and about twelve inches too short, so that she moved about restlessly to find a comfortable position. She had not waited to make the bed up properly, collecting only a couple of blankets as she sped past the linen cupboard at the top of the stairs. The rough wool tickled her and the hard ticking of the uncovered pillow scoured her cheek. After three or four abortive attempts, she gave up even trying to sleep and lay quietly in the darkness, listening to Philip's steady breathing and making plans. Plans in which Jerome Manfred figured, but only very briefly. She would use him, she decided, for just as long as it was convenient.

Towards morning she finally fell into an exhausted sleep. On the borders of it, hazy thoughts trickled through her mind. Why? He had given her several reasons for marrying her and she didn't believe any of them. He was using her in some way and for some purpose of his own, and she didn't think that consideration for Philip's orphaned state or a desire to have children of his own had anything to do with it. So he was using her; she couldn't quarrel with that because she proposed using him, didn't she? Tit for tat!

A discreet tap aroused her. It also roused Philip, who scrambled energetically out of his cot and bounced blithely on her chest.

'My daddy,' he demanded. 'Want my daddy!'

Kate was not feeling her best. A near sleepless night and a heavy but short sleep had brought on a depression so that the plans which she had made during the night now seemed ridiculous and unworkable. And she had started worrying again, so that when Philip started using her as a trampoline, she grew cross.

'He's not your daddy, darling. He's your uncle. You must call him Uncle—Uncle Jerome.'

Whatever else she might have said was cut off

abruptly by Philip's howl of wrath. 'My daddy, he is, he *is*!'

Kate sighed and closed her eyes. 'Philip darling,' she said between her teeth, 'the man is your uncle. Be quiet!' But her words fell on deaf ears, the little boy was crying tears of rage and pummelling her with chubby fists while he screamed defiantly:

'My daddy, my daddy, *my daddy*!'

His final yell was cut short and Kate felt the weight removed from her chest. She looked up at Jerome Manfred, who stood looking gigantic in the small room and holding Philip's threshing body easily in one hand. She watched in horror as he deliberately turned the child over and slapped his bottom hard before dropping him back in his cot. Anger rose in her so that she struggled out of the blankets which enveloped her.

'Don't you dare do that again!' Her eyes blazed and she made a move towards the cot, a move that was stopped by a hard hand about her arm.

'Leave him! What are you trying to do, spoil the child?'

'He's little more than a baby, he doesn't understand!' She tried to twist free and raised furious green eyes to the dark, enigmatic face above her. Her free arm swung in an arc at his face, but was caught before her hand could land on its objective and she felt herself shaken, and not gently.

'Kate! Every child needs discipline, Philip no less than any other.'

'He needs love. . . .' Her remark was cut short before she had a chance to tell him just what Philip needed and just what she would do if he ever laid a finger on the boy again.

'We'll continue this at another time,' he was curt. 'Get yourselves dressed.'

'Want Daddy to dress me!' Philip had been watching events with interested eyes.

'Aunt Kate will dress you.' Jerome Manfred hardly seemed to notice the interruption. 'And I'm not your daddy. You may call me Uncle.'

'Yes!' Philip smiled widely about it, and Kate blinked with surprise.

She made a rapid sortie down to the kitchen for a can of hot water and fled back upstairs with it, and after washing her own hands and face she started on the mammoth task of making Philip presentable, idly wondering how a three-year-old could collect so much dirt on his face during a night's repose. It was a considerable struggle to get him clean because recently Philip had decided that water had an injurious effect on his complexion and objected violently to anything more than two or three square inches around his mouth being soaped and rinsed. Kate emerged from the tussle victorious but flushed with effort and with her temper a little uncertain.

When she arrived in the kitchen, it was to find Jerome Manfred already there, washed, shaved and impeccably groomed. The kitchen table was also laid for breakfast, and her look of astonishment was noted.

'An electric shaver which plugs into the car battery,' he explained. 'It wasn't worth relighting the fire,' he gestured at the empty grate. 'We must leave as soon as possible. Whichever way we go, we have to take the Exeter bypass, and that means we lose time.'

Kate nodded as she lit the second ring of the cooker to heat the milk for Philip's cereal.

'We've not much packing, I didn't bring a lot,' she muttered as she pushed past him to remove the kettle which had started to whistle. Silently, she prayed that Philip would be good, would eat his cereal properly and not feed it in sloppy spoonsful to the puppy. The puppy! She turned back to Jerome Manfred, who stood making the kitchen look very crowded. 'Philip's puppy—I bought it for him. It's from a very good strain. I can't leave it here, there won't be anybody to feed it. It would starve.'

He raised an eyebrow. 'Bring it,' and he turned a dark grey, impersonal gaze on her; taking in her tweed skirt, woollen jumper, thickish stockings and sturdy, sensible shoes. It made her feel uncomfortable and she turned to the tiny fridge, speaking quickly.

'There's some bacon and eggs—would you like them? Because if you don't want them, they'll have to be thrown away, wasted, and I hate waste. I only have toast and Philip's not up to bacon yet, he'll have a boiled egg after his cereal.' Her voice came muffled from the fridge and when she straightened, her face was flushed from stooping.

'Go for a walk.' Philip spoke thickly through a mouthful of cereal. 'Go for a walk with my dog.'

Kate opened her mouth to answer, but found she was forestalled. Jerome was definite.

'No! Today we go for a drive in the car. Tomorrow you may take your dog for a walk.' Kate expected tears, but they were not forthcoming. Philip smiled his sweet, fat smile.

'O.K.,' he agreed angelically, and then, in case that should not be enough, 'Thank you.'

'And there's my car,' Kate muttered as she set Jerome's breakfast before him.

'The old Morris 1000,' he dismissed it with a careless wave of his hand. 'Leave it.'

'I'll do no such thing!' She was indignant. 'It's been a lovely old car, I've never had a moment's trouble with it and it took me nearly two years to pay for it. I'm not abandoning it like that.'

'You should have had a bank loan,' he pointed out. 'The interest charges wouldn't have been so high and you would have paid for it more quickly.'

'Mr Manfred,' her voice was icy, 'at the time when I bought that car, I was a very new, very naïve teacher, but I'd learned one thing about banks. The only time they're willing to give you a loan is when you can prove you don't need it, and I couldn't do that! I want my car.'

'Give me the keys when we get to London and I'll have it collected for you.' He spoke with his weary insolence as if he was becoming tired of humouring a particularly fractious child. Kate compressed her lips and turned her mind to other fractious thoughts.

'This cottage,' she looked around. 'I don't like leaving it like this. It will all have to be cleaned.' She wrinkled her nose in distaste at the blobs of cereal which Philip had been dropping for his puppy. 'Helen let it to me as a favour and it would be the height of ingratitude if I left it looking like a mess. Surely we could go tomorrow—there's no real reason why we have to go today, is there?'

'Yes, there is.' He was curt and frowning. 'Forget about the cottage,' he advised.

Kate shook her head in a determined fashion. 'Not good enough! Helen loves this place, she used to come here for holidays when she was a child, and besides, she could probably let it again straight away as soon as she knows I'm gone. It would have to be clean and habitable for that. You did say that her last exhibition wasn't a great success, didn't you? She'll need the money.' Her mouth firmed as she thought of unswept floors and the usual chaos left after a hurried departure. 'I'm not going to leave it looking as if a bomb's hit it,' she finished pugnaciously.

Jerome looked at her carefully. 'I appreciate your sense of loyalty, but it seems to get you into trouble more often than not, or haven't you noticed? Your misguided efforts at obtaining a large sum of money to help your sister should have been an example to you. If it was an example, you haven't learned by it. You didn't help matters then, did you? Within a year, things were back in the position they'd been in before you allowed yourself to be photographed for that girlie calendar. In fact, the only thing you really achieved was the possibility of destroying your own reputation. Happily, I was able to prevent that, but if you hadn't interfered, I couldn't have come threatening you, could I?'

Kate flushed. What he had said was quite true, although she found it difficult to admit, even to herself. But at the time, Shirley had been grateful. Yes, she was sure that Shirley had been grateful.

'That was my own fault.' She kept her eyes resolutely on the plate she was washing. 'We needed so much more money than I'd calculated and we were beginning to feel cramped; Shirley and I and the baby all in my little place. I thought, if we had a bigger flat. . . .'

'You thought Shirley would complain less?'

'No, not that at all.'

'Don't try to tell me that she didn't complain.' Jerome sounded disbelieving.

'Of course she complained!' She swung round, the dripping dish mop raised to emphasise her point. 'I couldn't expect her not to complain, could I? Theo had shown her an altogether different kind of life. She'd become used to luxury, to never having to think about trifles like phone bills, electricity bills and the rest of the cost of living. She'd grown used to lovely clothes and being able to buy anything which took her fancy and she'd become used to space, and in my little flat there wasn't enough room to swing a cat. Besides, there was the baby. I didn't blame her at all, if that's what you're thinking. It was different for me, I was out nearly all day, but Shirley was cooped up in my tiny place with a baby to look after and nobody to talk to. It was driving her mad! But we've strayed off the point, haven't we? The point I was making is this cottage—I will not leave it in a mess!'

'We will leave it in precisely one hour.' He glanced at his watch. 'We're going to London today, whether this house conforms to your domestic standards or not. To be even more precise, I'm taking Philip today. If you prefer to stay here, scrubbing floors,' he shrugged eloquently, 'you may do so.'

'But you need a wife—you said so,' she reminded him triumphantly.

He slanted a glance down at her and his eyes glittered. 'I can buy someone else, if I have to. Money, Kate, is the most potent aphrodisiac in the world!'

Checkmate again! She kept her face hidden while she tried to make plans, but her thoughts were dreary. Plans were useless if she became parted from Philip. Her only chance lay in being with the child.

'Very well.' She forced a smile and a brisk note in her voice as she wiped her hands on a towel. 'An hour, you said—then take Philip and the dog for a walk while I do what I can. They'll both need the exercise if they're going to be cooped up in a car all day and I can get through quite a lot in an hour.'

When they had gone, she stood at the window for a few minutes watching their retreating figures. A man, a boy and a dog! Philip's short, sturdy legs were pumping up and down as he tried to keep pace with the puppy, and Kate smiled tenderly at his little figure. Then he stopped and turned to say something to the man and the pale sunlight illuminated his round, plump face. So young, she thought, and wished vainly that he might never have to grow up, never have to lose the innocence of youth, never know how hard life could be. But the Manfred money would be a lovely cushion for him, and she cheered up at the thought. Philip would never be driven into doing unpleasant things just for the sake of money, and if she stayed with him and made sure that his values were the right ones. . . .

With a start, she realised that she was wasting time and started rushing around, sweeping floors, dusting, stripping beds and thanking heaven that she had brought her own bedlinen with her. She made a pile of all the dirty stuff and gave a swift look of contentment at the linen cupboard; everything in it was clean and orderly. She cleaned out the fridge, packing everything into a plastic bag before putting it in the bin—refuse collection on Bodmin Moor was a chancy business—and then she went off to pack suitcases before she washed and changed. It was one thing she missed; the bathroom and the supply of constant hot water which went with it. She had enjoyed the tin bath in front of the kitchen fire after Philip had been put to bed at night. After the first week, to sit in a bath, the warmth of the fire on her face and shoulders and protected from draughts by towels spread on the clothes airer, had seemed the height of luxury, but then came the letdown. After towelling herself dry, there was no chance of sliding into her nightwear and trotting off to bed, warm and relaxed. The dratted bath had to be emptied and put away, which took nearly all the pleasure out of the proceedings.

This morning there was no time for a bath and no hot water either. She shook the kettle; there was still a

little hot water left in it and she was vicious about turning off the taps on the gas cylinder. One hour Jerome
had allowed her, and she had already used nearly three
quarters of it. With a sigh of resignation she poured out
the small quantity of hot water remaining in the kettle
and made do with that. Her clothes were laid ready on
the stripped bed and she hurried into them—a grey
flannel skirt, a cream wool polo-necked jumper and a
neat navy blue blazer-style jacket.

She was just tying the laces of her practical, sturdy
shoes when she heard the bang of the garden gate. A
quick glance in the mirror assured her that her chestnut
coil of hair was smooth and that the small quantity of
make-up she wore was adequate but no more. This was
Kate Forrest looking back at her from the mirror, good
old, sensible Kate! Kate who taught at school, who liked
to sit out in the garden in the summer and who curled
up by the fire in the winter with a good book. Kate who
liked the gentle things and to whom romantic and unpleasant things did not happen.

She nodded calmly at her reflection in the mirror.
That was the way to treat this bizarre situation, she
decided—with calm, practical common sense. It did no
good to lose one's temper or to indulge in histrionics or
even to contemplate gory acts with a carving knife.
Tempers and drama were out! She wouldn't kill Jerome
Manfred or bring him to the brink of ruin. She wouldn't
fight with him, perhaps she wouldn't even try to take
Philip and escape. She would stay put, become once
again Kate Forrest, she would be a good, obedient wife
and as dull as ditchwater. And she would bore him to
death!

CHAPTER THREE

THEY arrived in London in the early twilight of the February evening and Jerome drove straight to his flat. Kate had enlivened the journey with several bouts of calm, good common sense. The first was when the puppy was sick, the second was when the puppy was sick again and the third, fourth and fifth times, when Philip was car-sick, chocolate-sick and plain bored sick. The inside of the Ferrari had suffered considerably in consequence and Kate had watched Jerome's face become steadily more rigid with distaste. At the beginning of the journey, she had offered to sit in the back and keep the other two passengers amused, but her offer had been refused. So the mess in the car was his own fault, she consoled herself, and she was glad of it. She wished there was twice as much!

She also diverted her mind from her problems by making bets with herself as to the probable size and splendour of the flat. It would be the sort of place, she decided, where Noelle Lowe would be completely at home—huge, modernistically furnished in white leather, chrome and smoked glass with everything built in. It would not be the sort of place which Philip or the puppy would appreciate, or herself either, for that matter. She would encourage both Philip and the puppy to jump all over the furniture and sweep ornaments from low tables on to the floor with as much broken glass as possible! Yes, the whole place would be very elegant, very sophisticated and very expensive—and she won all her bets.

But it wasn't Noelle Lowe who entered the flat, it was no-nonsense Kate Forrest, who liked cosy, chintz-covered armchairs and the mellow shine of old wood, so after a quick look round, she rejoined Philip in the kitchen. It was a superbly laid out and equipped kitchen and she surveyed it with a faint smile on her lips.

Philip had woken up when they arrived and was now seated at the kitchen table, overtired, fretful and petulant.

'Don't want it!' He pushed at his dish and Kate watched with pleasure as the piece of delicate china containing nourishing soup skittered across the smoked glass table top and shattered on the immaculate Italian floor tiles, sending globules of soup spattering over the floor and the nearby walls.

Firm hands on her shoulders moved her to one side as Jerome passed her, filled another bowl with soup and placed it on the table in front of the little boy.

'Eat it!'

Philip stared at his uncle warily, obviously assessing the opposition, and then smiled angelically.

'O.K.! And drink my cocoa,' he added generously.

When Philip was safely tucked up in bed and Kate had cleared and cleaned the bathroom—it was surprising how much mess a boy and a puppy could make in a bathroom, especially when they were both jumping in and out of the bath and rushing round the floor—she returned to the kitchen, flushed and out of breath. Jerome suggested dinner, and Kate looked at him pityingly.

'Apart from not being dressed for dinner in a res-taurant and not having any suitable clothes with me into which I could change; I can't leave Philip. He might wake and want me. You'll have to go by yourself.'

Jerome's smile was not pleasant. 'You don't give up easily, do you? But as I said before, I don't trust you, Kate. You are, I think, a woman of infinite resource.' He stood negligently by the door, looking at her, his eyes mocking. 'I can see quite well that you aren't dressed for dinner out, but there's ample food here and I'm sure you aren't devoid of the housewifely arts. The preparation of a simple meal for two persons is surely not beyond your capabilities, is it? Then after we've eaten, we can have the discussion I've been promising.'

'I thought we'd been into all that.'

'No, not all of it, but after dinner, we will.' It was phrased as a polite statement, but to Kate it sounded very much like a threat.

She had never felt less like cooking in her life and even all the gadgetry and the microwave oven woke no spark of enthusiasm in her breast. She grumbled silently about men who said 'We will have dinner' and then went away to another room and left a woman to get on with it. The freezer was full, however, and she delved among its neat packages and dragged out steak and vegetables to thaw and then worked off some of her bad temper in battering the steaks with a serrated mallet. All the time she was frying the steak, sautéing the potatoes, cooking the peas and whipping up a cheese-cake, she thought. She thought about what she would do, what she would say and how she would say it, and then moved on to her priorities.

Her first priority was to get in touch with Gerald. She had changed her mind about escaping; she would do it if she could, and she couldn't do it on her own. She would need somewhere to hide, and the only place available was her own flat—Noelle Lowe's flat, she corrected herself—and that would be the first place where Jerome would look. What she wanted was somewhere remote, the Lake District or Scotland, perhaps. Then she grinned to herself wryly. In such a place, she and Philip would stick out like a couple of sore thumbs. She would be much better here in London, in a very densely populated part where people were too busy to bother about who lived

in the room above or below. A bedsitter would do for
the time being, and Gerald could surely find her that.

She then thought up several smart and tart answers
to use if Jerome asked the right questions, and when the
food was ready, and the table laid, she went off to the
bedroom to change. She peeped through the communicating door at Philip and crept softly to his bedside. He
was asleep, flat on his back, with an expression of an-
gelic innocence on his face and his puppy curled up
beside him and making a dreadful mess of the thick
satin coverlet. Kate bent to tuck the covers more closely
about the boy and dropped a soft kiss on his cheek
while her hand went to stroke the black curls which
clustered on his forehead. He was a beautiful boy, she
thought; well worth any sacrifice she might have to
make—and she would make any sacrifice to remain with
him. He was all she had now that Shirley was gone, her
only link, and she was not going to be parted from him,
not even if it meant marrying Jerome Manfred! But it
hadn't come to that, not yet. She had promised, but it was
a promise extracted under duress, so she would have no
compunction in breaking it. If she had the opportunity!

Softly, so as not to disturb the sleeping child, she
rummaged through her suitcases for a change of clothes.
The selection available was strictly limited and they were
all 'Kate' clothes with not a wisp of glamour anywhere.
She sighed as she realised that Helen had been right,
she had grown used to lovely clothes, used to wearing
them and looking good in them. At the cottage, she
hadn't bothered much what she had worn, she had been
too worried, too full of the perpetual nagging fear of
being tracked down. But now the worst that she had
feared, being found by the Manfreds, had happened and
she hadn't had time to start worrying about her new
problems yet. Come to think of it, she hadn't yet worked

out what her new problems would be.

Finally she settled for a fine wool skirt in tobacco brown, a bronzy green silk shirt and the only elegant shoes she had with her, dressy courts, high-heeled and slim in bronze patent leather. The reflection which stared back at her from the mirror was a minor shock. Four months in a remote cottage, out of reach of a hairdresser, had transformed her smooth, sophisticated hairdo into an over-long, over-thick mess. She regretted having washed it, but the bathroom in this apartment had been more than she could resist; after four months of tin baths in front of the kitchen fire, Jerome Manfred's luxuriously appointed bath had drawn her like a magnet. She had wallowed in sybaritic luxury, up to her chin in delicately perfumed water, and it had seemed sinful not to wash her hair at the same time, so she had lathered and rinsed until the chestnut mass squeaked between her fingers. Now the short ends were curling about her temples and on the nape of her neck, refusing to lie smoothly, and the rest of her thick mane had an ungovernable air. Resolutely she reached for her brush and started methodically to tame it.

Kate laid out her few remaining bits of make-up on the dressing table and surveyed the scanty collection with grim satisfaction. They would have done for Kate Forrest in a cottage on Bodmin Moor, but here, in London, in this luxury apartment, they were woefully inadequate. She shrugged to herself. There was nobody to see her here except Jerome Manfred, and he had seen her in the cottage—and in any case, she didn't care what he thought. It might be a good idea to make herself look as repulsive as possible. If he thought he was marrying Noelle Lowe or even having dinner with her, he was in for a rude awakening and a severe disappointment!

He didn't appear to be disappointed when she joined

him in the dining area where he was inspecting her pre-
parations. He seemed . . . nothing! There was no expression on his face, his features were cold and impassive
and his eyes hooded and unreadable. He looked down
at her, one sweeping glance taking in Kate.

'If you were expecting Noelle,' she was belligerent,
'I'd better tell you now so that you won't have any
wrong ideas for the future. That lady only existed for
the photographers. The person you see standing before
you is me, Kate Forrest, ex-schoolteacher. This is the
way I look, the way I like to look. Take it or leave it!'

His eyes slid down over her body and she felt the hot
blood in her cheeks and a throb of fear in her veins. It
was as if he had stripped her and was assessing the
smooth, shapely body underneath.

'There's a lot of Noelle Lowe left,' he murmured. 'I
mean the basic material on which the girl was built. I
can do without that smooth, egglike face with the
features painted on so exquisitely and I can do without the
sexy clothes which clung in all the right places. You're a
fool, Kate, if you insist that there were two different
people, Kate Forrest and Noelle Lowe. Stop deceiving
yourself. Noelle never existed at all, she was only ever
Kate, dressed up and wearing a painted mask on her face.'

'And there you're wrong!' She struggled with the ties
of a gay plastic apron, going red in the face with effort.
'I am Kate Forrest, I invented Noelle and she existed all
right! She did things which Kate would never have done
and I disliked her very much. Four months ago I ended
her existence. She didn't even think like me!'

There was a quirk of grim amusement about his
mouth as he carefully sorted out the tangled tapes of
the apron and drew it from her. 'You don't need this.
Sit down, Kate, and stop worrying. Whichever woman I
find, I shall call her "Kate".'

She subsided into the chair he had pulled out for her and carefully ignored the glass of sherry which he offered. She looked at the counter where the bottles of table wine stood ready and her lips firmed. Whatever happened, she was going to drink nothing but water. If he thought he was going to get her into his bed in a drunken stupor, then he was very much mistaken. Perhaps when dinner was over and she had given him his coffee, she would make herself a mug of cocoa. Mugs of cocoa were earthy things, there was nothing even vaguely romantic or seductive about them. A man would find it hard to indulge in a passionate interlude with a woman who was clutching a mug of cocoa!

They ate the meal in silence, and for Kate it seemed to go on for ever. Jerome didn't seem to consider it necessary to indulge in light conversation, she supposed that he wasn't used to it. He probably worked on the presumption that women were necessary to satisfy certain of his appetites, and for that, they didn't have to talk! When it was at last over, she rose swiftly and began to roll up the sleeves of her shirt. As she did so, she moved purposefully towards the sink. If luck was with her, she would take at least an hour to wash up and then she would get her mug of cocoa and go straight to bed, thereby postponing any discussion until the morning at the earliest. Her hand was just reaching towards the hot tap when Jerome's voice cut across her self-congratulatory mood.

'Our discussion, Kate,' she was reminded.

'I'll clear up first and get everything tidy.' She turned an artificially bright smile on him as she put the plug in the sink and squirted in far too much washing up liquid. 'I couldn't sit talking with all this clutter to be cleared,' she waved at the table, draining board and counter where used crockery, cutlery, glasses and pans were stacked. 'Even if I was in another room and couldn't see the mess, I'd not be able to concentrate on a word you said, not until it was all cleared away and the place tidied up. It's one of the unpleasant things about schoolteachers, we generally turn into fusspots. We can't help it, I've seen it happen to so many of us. I think it must be an occupational hazard.'

She was still babbling brightly and inanely when she heard a faint sound of exasperation behind her and firm hands shifted her bodily to one side as he passed her and started to load the dishwasher.

'There!' She continued her chattering in a cheerful vein. 'That's what living in a cottage on Bodmin Moor does for you, that and being a member of the lower orders, of course. When there's work to be done, we automatically use our hands. We're not used to gadgets or servants, you see, and it's very hard for us to adjust. Some of us never. . . .'

There was no more time for her to explain further what some of the lower orders would never be able to adjust to, because a firm hand, a relentless hand, came about her arm.

'Now we'll go into the sitting room,' he said urbanely as he dragged her through the door.

Kate sat primly, her ankles neatly crossed and her hands lying loosely in her lap while she turned an uninterested face to him.

'Noelle?' He made it a question. 'How much of her reputation was deserved? She was seen about with a great many escorts, some of them were a trifle, shall we say, unsavoury. At one time it was impossible to find a paper or magazine which didn't picture her dining with some man and apparently on quite intimate terms with him.'

'It was a con.' She was terse. 'They wanted to launch products using my face and they explained to me that for the campaigns to be a success, my face had to be better known, brought out of the ivory tower of the studio and shown to be human.' She made a moue of distaste. 'You'd be surprised at the number of wealthy and quite eligible men who are willing to act as an escort when there's a bit of publicity about. Of course,' her mouth grew bitter, 'even though the meals were paid for and the drinks and theatre tickets were free, it was surprising to me how high a value they put on their time. Most of them thought that an evening with Noelle didn't end until nine the next morning, or that it shouldn't! A lot of them were very hard to convince.' She smiled a bitter smile of reminiscence. 'One member of the jet set found himself lumbered with Philip, who was cutting teeth at the time, and with Shirley who was having hysterics because she was being kept awake by his crying. It served him right! He shouldn't have assumed that he was God's little gift to the female sex.'

Jerome nodded as if he was satisfied and went on to detail arrangements.

'Today is Monday, tomorrow I shall apply for a licence and we shall be married on Saturday morning at a small church nearby. No!' he raised his hand to stop her comments, 'it will be done as quickly as possible under the circumstances, but unfortunately for you, there will have to be some show and publicity. Afterwards there'll be a reasonably large reception, but the gentlemen of the Press will be barred from that. My mother will make all the arrangements. I don't need any information from you for the actual application for the licence, I have it all already.'

'Your private spies!' Kate made them sound like the Gestapo.

'Precisely. I know your date of birth and where you were born, I know your mother's maiden name and the profession of your father, so there's no need for any more nonsense about the "lower orders". Since when has a professor of English Literature earned his bread with sweat?'

'My father's hobby was bricklaying,' she told him sweetly. 'He often said that he was a better bricklayer than a professor.' She choked back the rest of the sarcastic remark which she had been going to make so that it died before it reached her lips. She was going to be calm, placid Kate, she remembered; sensible and boring! 'Is that all?' she enquired, 'because, if it is, I think I'll ask you to excuse me. It's been a long upsetting day and I slept badly last night. I'm feeling very tired.'

'One or two things more.' He was watching her closely and she felt like a mouse being stalked by a hungry cat. 'After the wedding, we shall take a short honeymoon. I'm afraid it will have to be short, I have some business coming up. Where would you like to go?'

Kate yawned pointedly at him. 'Anywhere, I suppose. I'm not greatly interested.' She didn't sound interested. 'Somewhere Philip will enjoy, somewhere warm and sunny, it's not been a very nice winter for him. As long as he's happy, I don't give a row of pins where we go.'

'I hadn't envisaged taking Philip.' It was the growl of the big cat just before it unsheathed its claws.

'Not take Philip!' Calm, sensible Kate nearly vanished in a blaze of indignation. 'What did you propose to do with him, leave him in a luggage office labelled "To Be Called For"? He's a little boy, not a parcel, and where I go, he goes.'

'Not on your honeymoon.' Jerome contemplated the burning tip of his cigarette.

'Then there won't be a honeymoon.' She was defiant. 'You can take us where we're going to live and we'll stay there. It will save time, money and all the bother of travelling. It will be better for Philip anyway, he's at an age when he needs a settled home. The cottage was all right, but the weather was bad and I wasn't the best of company, although I tried hard not to let it show. I was nervous about being found. Oh, and by the way, don't suggest that we live in this apartment, because I refuse. It's not at all the sort of place in which to bring up children.' She cast a glance around the modernistically immaculate room. 'It looks like the waiting room in a private clinic.'

He ignored this last remark and the several preceding it, fastening on an earlier one. 'So, the weather was bad, you were nervous all the time and I think you were running short of money.'

'We had enough,' she glared at him. 'We could have managed for quite a long time, until April at least, and then I had the offer of a temporary post at a school in Sussex, so don't think you've saved us from starvation, because you haven't!'

'But that's all over now.' He sounded serene. 'You're marrying me and we're having a honeymoon, and I don't want Philip to come with us.'

Kate closed her eyes to shut out the red mist of temper that was floating between her and this arrogant, impossible man. She drew a deep breath and forced her voice to be steady.

'Where I go,' she said tonelessly and emphatically, 'Philip goes. Have I made that clear to you, Mr Manfred?'

'We seem to have reached an impasse.' He sounded unruffled and his face gave nothing away.

Kate sat quite still and looked at him steadily. Inwardly she was shaking, but outwardly she was calm. There was nothing in her but a fierce pride and an even fiercer determination. She would not beg, neither would she give way. He could think what he liked of her, she didn't care! If he wanted to think her all kinds of a trollop, he was welcome to do so. His opinion of her was of no consequence, it didn't matter to her, not one iota, but she was *not* being parted from Philip! She drew a deep breath which thinned her nostrils.

'Of course we've reached an impasse,' she was scornful. 'What did you expect? That I should get down on my knees and thank you humbly for the honour you're doing me?' Her voice developed a bitter note. 'I'm marrying you, Mr Manfred, so that I can keep Philip with me, and as I said before, I don't consider it an honour. I consider your offer an insult. You evidently don't have much of an opinion of me—I'll go along with that, I don't have much of an opinion of myself. Like the rest of the quite ordinary members of the human race, I'm far from perfect and I admit it. I may have done some stupid things, I *have* done some stupid things, but my motives were good. I don't care what you or anybody else thinks about me, I've kept my integrity— *and* I didn't have a hedge of money a mile high to hide behind. Whereas you, Mr Manfred, are shop-soiled, so don't think you're doing me any favours. Under normal conditions, I wouldn't touch you with a ten-foot bargepole!' Kate uncrossed her ankles and stood up. 'Now, if you'll excuse me. . . .'

He rose with her to stand over her and she received the impression of menace and hard held temper. 'Kate, you're becoming shrewish and obstinate. Come here.' He held out his hand.

She backed off. 'No!'

'Then pack your things and I'll ring for a taxi. You can go.'

She stood silent, feeling as though she had been drenched with a bucket of ice water. 'Philip,' she said through lips stiff with fear.

'Is asleep. I see no need to wake him so that you can say goodbye.'

'You don't mean it,' she whispered.

'Try me,' he advised. 'Come here.'

When she stood within the circle of his arm, he looked down at her mockingly. 'Now do you understand? I said I wanted a wife I could control, and that's what I intend to have. You're vulnerable, Kate, and I hold the means of controlling you. I have Philip and the negatives. You want Philip and you want to go back to being a schoolteacher. You can stay with Philip, on my terms, but if you leave, I'm afraid you'll have no chance of teaching. I'll circulate those negatives to every education authority in the country. Who would employ you then, do you think?'

His arm tightened about her and he lowered his head to hers, his mouth forcing a response from her lips. When he raised his head, Kate stood very still while his fingers coolly unfastened the buttons of her shirt and pushed it over her shoulder. She gasped as his hand closed over her breast and shuddered as he enquired mockingly, 'How long was that bargepole you wouldn't touch me with, Kate?'

Her eyes were glittering with unshed tears and her lower lip was swollen, but she faced him, doing all she could to conceal the tremors which shook her.

'If you've humiliated me enough for one night,' she muttered, 'I'll ask you to excuse me. I'm very tired.' At the door, she turned back to see him unconcernedly lighting another cigarette. His complete unconcern swept away the hold she had put on her tongue.

'Goodnight—and the bargepole was ten foot long!' She snapped off the words sharply.

'Go to bed, Kate.' His voice was noncommittal.

And I bet, she thought with a dull satisfaction, that's

the first time in years anybody has told him what they think of him, and she carefully locked the bedroom door. She had examined the flat when they had arrived, not completely but sufficiently to familiarise herself with the broad outlines. There were only two bedrooms, Philip was in one and she was occupying the other. Mr Jerome Manfred was going to have to sleep on the couch! But it was a comfortable couch. She made a face as one part of her, the bad part, expressed a vehement wish that the fat squabs and cushions had been stuffed with concrete!

In the bedroom, she rooted through her case for night-wear and gathering that and her toilet bag, let herself into the bathroom through the connecting door. With shaking fingers she locked it and the door into the corridor and stood contemplating herself in the mirror. She was astonished to find that she looked quite normal and that nothing of her inward perturbation was showing.

The shower looked inviting and she bundled up her hair under a plastic cap and divested herself of her clothes. She was still nervous, but here, locked in the bathroom, she could be as nervous as she liked. There was no need to keep up a stolid front in here, by herself. She could shake all over like a jelly and it didn't matter as long as she could present a cool, calm face when she was with Jerome Manfred. Nothing mattered as long as he didn't know what an abysmal coward she really was. She was going into this marriage with her eyes open, knowing that she could expect no mercy from him. He would take her with as little thought as he would take a glass of brandy with his coffee. She could only expect the worst and it would have to be tolerated. She closed her eyes to squeeze back the tears. It was for Philip!

She choked down a frantic desire to unlock the door and run whimpering to him, offering him complete con-

trol of the boy just as long as he would let her go and
not force her. She could feel the perspiration wet and
cold on her forehead and she stood rigidly while the
needle jets of the shower played on her back. It would
do no good, anyway, not if she begged on her knees.
Jerome had those negatives and he would use them, of
that she was certain. If she left here, left Philip with
him, what was there for her? Only a return to being
Noelle Lowe. She was trapped!

So this was fear! Whichever way she turned, she ran
into a brick wall—no, not a brick wall; she ran into the
hard, uncompromising block which was Jerome Manfred. This was fear? She jeered at herself. Wait until
Saturday night, my girl. Then you'll have something to
be really afraid about!

With cold hands she let herself back into the bedroom
and tiptoed through into the other room where Philip
was sleeping soundly. She looked down at him fondly;
he was worth it, he was worth anything, and with a sigh
she went back to her own bed and slid beneath the
covers, leaving the bedside lamp switched on in case he
should wake during the night and be frightened in these
unfamiliar surroundings.

Kate slept very well considering all she had on her
mind, and she woke to pale sunshine and Philip bouncing on her chest.

'Uncle,' he was demanding her attention. 'Uncle
knocked.'

Kate stared at him as she caught herself together. She
was not at the cottage, she was here in London, in
Jerome Manfred's flat, and if what she remembered was
not a nightmare, on Saturday she would be Mrs Jerome
Manfred. She closed her eyes against the thought. Last
night she had known it, but it hadn't seemed as real as
it did in the cold light of day.

Again came the quiet knock, and putting Philip to one side, she slid out of bed and hurried into her dressing gown, a most unglamorous garment of camel-coloured wool which she had packed for its warmth rather than its looks. She opened the bedroom door and he was standing outside, a cup of tea in his hand.

'Good morning.' He was as expressionless as the Sphinx. 'You slept well?'

'Thank you,' Kate heard herself being curt as she accepted the tea.

'Perhaps you could hurry,' he suggested blandly. 'We have a lot to do. . . .'

'You don't need me for any of it,' she cut across his words and watched him fending off Philip's advances. 'You said last night that you didn't need me, that you had all the information you required.'

'But you will come with me, Kate.' The remote, half smile curved his mouth. 'I still don't trust you, remember? I prefer to keep you in sight at all times until Saturday, you and the boy. After that there'll be no need. Come to breakfast.' He hoisted Philip under his arm and stalked off towards the kitchen.

Within fifteen minutes Kate joined him, dressed and ready for battle.

'I don't trust you, either.' She was unsmiling. 'You want Philip!' She was interrupted by the little boy's howl. 'You've made his milk too hot,' she scolded, and with an unsteady hand she diluted the contents of the cereal bowl with cold milk and restored the spoon to Philip's small, fat fingers.

'Then we shall watch each other.' Jerome waited while she seated herself. 'You're too close now to your friend Gerald Twyford. A telephone call and he'll be charging to your rescue on his pretty pale pink charger, ready to tear you from the grasp of the filthy capitalists.'

Kate folded her mouth firmly and remembered the bit about boring him to death while she mulled over the shadowy outlines of a plan. First, she must get to a telephone, and she retired into deeper silence to think about it.

They left the flat at ten o'clock and Kate's protest about leaving without clearing up died on her lips. Jerome was as calm and cold as ever.

'There's a maid and cleaning service.' He grasped her arm painfully and directed her to the bedroom. 'We're going shopping,' he announced. 'I to get a marriage licence and you, I presume, for some clothes for the wedding both for yourself and the boy. Also you'll need some other clothes, things suitable for Southern Italy. I have a villa of sorts in Calabria and we shall go there, since you refuse to go without the child and I refuse to go where the gentlemen of the Press might find me, on honeymoon with not only a bride but a three-year-old boy who resembles me closely. I shouldn't be embarrassed, but I don't care to have you stumbling over explanations and trying to convince them that Philip is your nephew! The place in Calabria is primitive, but it will have to do.'

Kate raised her eyebrows. Jerome Manfred had given in! He didn't treat it as giving in, of course. He made it sound as though he was doing her the most terrific favour. Arrogant swine, she swore to herself. But Calabria! That was down in the toe or heel of Italy, she wasn't sure which, and she was not going to parade her ignorance for him to treat her to one of his contemptuous smiles.

'Why do we have to go away at all?' She wrinkled her brow as they went down in the lift. 'I don't like the thought of taking a little boy abroad. Suppose he was ill? Young children catch all sorts of things and I can't recall whether he was ever vaccinated. I'd rather stay in England. You said the place there was primitive, suppose that the water supply isn't pure? It easily could be in primitive places where there's no proper drainage.'

'It was you who specified somewhere warm, remember?' Jerome was aggravatingly unmoved. 'Somewhere, you said, where the boy could enjoy himself, somewhere warm. I've merely done the best I can to accede to your wishes. Now, I'm sorry, but it's all arranged and it's too late for second thoughts. Perhaps you won't be so hasty in future. And the boy has been vaccinated. He was done when Theo proposed to take him to Crete with them.'

'When Theo proposed to take him!' Kate raised her lip in a delicate sneer. 'Your brother couldn't have cared less whether he had a son or not!'

Jerome walked them across the pavement and after bestowing Philip in the back of the car, pushed Kate in through the front passenger door with a far from gentle hand. He walked round the car and got in himself and sat with his hands on the steering wheel, staring bleakly through the windscreen. 'Are you deaf as well as blind, Kate?' It was almost a snarl. 'Who is it that Philip is always asking for? Not his mother! Yes, Theo proposed to take the boy with him to Crete. You can believe it or not as you please.'

CHAPTER FOUR

MUCH later, when Kate looked back on that week, she could only find a confused blur in her memory. Things had happened because Jerome Manfred made them happen. He started the wheels in motion and, once turning, they ground on relentlessly and Kate found herself a victim of the system.

She was very foggy about everything, although some episodes stood out clear in her mind, as when, on that first day in London, they had done their shopping together.

In the register office they had sat waiting side by side on very hard chairs, and Kate had been hard put to it to control Philip, who had grown bored with the delay and wanted to enliven the process by pretending that he was a train. His shuffling feet and his constant, noisy whoo-whoos had caused raised eyebrows and deprecating looks from the other people waiting, and he refused to pay any attention to Kate's remonstrances. It was not until Jerome rose, captured him and sat him firmly on a chair that peace reigned once more. Then in the Registrar's office, a very untidy office, she thought, she sat mute while Jerome gave the required information. It still didn't seem real and she was astounded to find that, instead of paying attention, all she could think of was that she was terribly thirsty and would have given her eye teeth for a cup of tea. She thought of the tea as she listened to Jerome and the Registrar. It would be in a dumpy little pot and would come out of the spout in a clear golden stream.

Outside the building, the desire for tea didn't disappear, it grew, so that she was forced to turn to him.

'Could we go somewhere and have a cup of tea?' She ventured the question and he had nodded quite amiably. He had frowned at the sticky cake which Philip had chosen for himself and replaced it with something plainer and had checked Philip's howl of anguish with a quelling look. At her third cup, he had looked at her.

'If you're ready,' he indicated Philip's wriggles, 'I think we should continue with our business. Harrods, I think.'

Several times, while she sorted through dresses, Kate was aware of his eyes on her and she hurriedly gathered up a pile and went off to the fitting room to try them on. They were all very plain day dresses and she eventually chose one in a cream wool, softly draped and with a matching, loose coat trimmed with coffee-coloured braid. He inspected her choice carefully.

'It won't do, Kate.' He shook his head. 'The wedding is to be in a church and my mother will expect you to be dressed traditionally. Something long and flowing with a train and a veil. My mother likes traditional things.'

'Your mother isn't getting married,' she told him brusquely, 'I am, and I refuse to dress up for this mockery, nor,' she added, 'have I any intention of promising to either love, honour or obey you. Why couldn't we have had a civil ceremony and cut out all this hypocrisy?' She hardly troubled to lower her voice, speaking in her normally clear tones, and was aware that the saleswoman was listening avidly. Jerome was aware of it too, for he caught her arm and let his fingers close around it painfully.

'Pick up your packages, Kate.' He smiled down at her lovingly for the saleswoman's benefit and continued in a lower voice while maintaining the smile. 'You will be properly dressed for this wedding, and if you won't choose something adequate, then it will be chosen for you, and you will wear it if I have to dress you in it myself.'

She smiled back at him, a smile of saccharine sweetness. 'A hat next, I think, darling,' she purred, and marched off to the millinery department. Part way through the business of choosing a hat, she became quite enthusiastic and found herself searching for something which would be just right—and then she remembered. She paused before the mirror with a cream hat in either hand and closed her eyes. It wasn't a matter of buying what she wanted or what she liked. It didn't matter whether she loved or hated it, she would never wear any of it again, she wouldn't even be able to look at it. It would all have to be either given away or burned. Personally, she was in favour of burning it all, in a public place and with as much smoke as possible, either that or cutting it all into very small pieces with a sharp pair of scissors.

She had one very bad moment when she had tried to phone Gerald. Jerome was in the small room which he used as an office and he had shut the door firmly, leaving her to mooch around the flat on her own, so she had crept silently to the bedroom and picked up the handset of the extension by the bed. There had been a faint burring sound, and with shaking fingers she had dialled Gerald's number and waited. She did not have to wait long. Jerome's voice came over the wire, clear in her ear. 'That number is unobtainable to you, Kate.' Vexed beyond all reason, she had flung the phone on the floor, locked herself in the bathroom and shouted every swear word she could think of, like a litany.

The struggle over the honeymoon continued. Kate refused to budge an inch. She didn't want to go to

Calabria, she didn't want to go anywhere!

'You talk about a honeymoon,' she turned on him, distaste in every line of her body and thick on her tongue. 'A honeymoon! Is that what you call it? Honeymoons are romantic things, for lovers. Find another name for it!'

Nothing stirred in the immobility of his face. 'According to what I've read, it used to be a period during which a couple came to know each other better so that when they returned they could take up life again among their acquaintances without embarrassment. We will use the period in that way. You will come to know me better and I shall learn a little more about you. Whether it will be romantic or not, I couldn't say, but we *will* be lovers, Kate. I'm looking forward to knowing more about you.'

'There's nothing more to know about me,' she snapped. 'I'm not a very complex person. When I'm happy, I laugh, when I'm miserable, I cry, and when I'm in a temper, I throw things about—and candidly, I don't want to know you any better than I already do. I'd be much happier if I didn't know you at all! Let me go, Mr Manfred. Let me and Philip go, I'll go back to teaching and Philip will be well looked after, I promise you that. This marriage, it's a farce and you know it, so why insist on it? In a couple of months, you'll be bored to tears and wanting a divorce. I'm not your type, you should know that.'

'You never stop trying, do you?' His voice held a note of wonder and something almost like reluctant admiration. 'No, we'll be married as I've planned—and don't build your hopes on the thought of a farcical marriage or a quick divorce. The marriage will not be a farce and I don't believe in divorce. If a man can't be happy with one woman. . . .'

'You won't be happy with me,' she broke in threaten-
ingly.

'Threats, Kate?'

On Wednesday evening, Mrs Manfred made a stun-
ning entrance into the flat. Kate drew Philip closer to
her and blinked with surprise. Beautiful, she thought,
admiring the fresh, clear complexion, the rather faded
blue eyes which were still magnificent and the silvery
fair hair which curled naturally over the lady's well
shaped head and round her very pretty ears. Mrs
Manfred was elegant, poised and very sure of herself,
besides being a grande dame of the first order. She was,
in fact, just as Shirley had described—and yet not as
Shirley had described. There was a merriment about the
lady, but Kate could detect no malice.

'Philip,' the lady cooed. 'Don't you remember me?
I'm Grandmama.' Philip buried his head in Kate's lap
and refused to show his face. Sensibly, Mrs Manfred
ignored this excessive shyness and turned to Kate. 'So
you're Kate!'

Kate eyed her rather frostily and said 'Yes' in a for-
bidding tone.

'And you're going to marry Jerome.' Mrs Manfred
whirled around to her son. 'It's all rather rushed, isn't
it, but I'm glad we're to have a nice wedding for a
change. Theo's was a hole-and-corner affair. I knew
you'd have better taste. Is there any special reason for
the hurry? I only ask because if there isn't, I do wish
you'd do it properly, at home. A proper wedding, in
Derbyshire, one with all the trimmings,' she wheedled.
'White satin and lace—Kate's too big for tulle—a big
reception at home where I can do things in style. It's
what I've always wanted for you. A girl only gets
married once, after all, so why don't you make it mem-
orable? Give Kate something to look back on, flowers,

bells and the choir singing "The Voice that Breathed o'er Eden". Give us all a treat.'

'There will be a church wedding, Mother, but it will be in London.' Jerome looked down at his mother with a wry kindness. 'There will also be flowers and bells. I hadn't thought of the choir or "The Voice that Breathed".' He glanced sideways at Kate, an eyebrow quirked. She shook her head emphatically. 'No,' he murmured, 'I don't think Kate is in an Eden frame of mind. And besides,' he continued smoothly, his face a study in non expression, 'Kate dislikes publicity almost as much as I do. It will make less of an impact in a quiet, small London church.'

Mrs Manfred sniffed down her long straight nose. 'You'll get publicity whether you want it or not. Millionaires always do.'

Kate sat silent, taking no part in the conversation and trying to make sense of her feelings. This was the woman whom she had been hating for over three years, yet there was nothing objectionable about her. Perhaps she had shown Shirley another side of her personality. Philip had raised his head slightly and was peeping at his grandmother from one eye which he was masking with his pudgy little fingers. Kate stroked his head gently and waited for Jerome to say something.

'Thank you, Mother, for the offer, but I don't think we could move Kate in this matter. She has a very low opinion of us.'

'Culled from that flibbertigibbet sister of hers, I suppose.' Mrs Manfred sniffed again and turned to Kate. 'I speak my mind, always have done. You and Jerome are getting married, are you so ashamed of it that you have to slink in and out of a little London church?'

Kate raised her chin and looked straight into the faded blue eyes. 'Yes!' she said firmly. 'Under normal

circumstances, nothing would induce me to marry your
son, but he's blackmailing me into it—he leaves me no
choice. I want to bring Philip up and this is the only
way he'll let me do it.'

Mrs Manfred laughed. It wasn't a titter of a laugh or
a polite tinkle, it was a deep belly laugh, full of mirth.
'Just like his father—and like me too, in a way. He'll be
a damned uncomfortable man to live with, too fond of
getting his own way. I like his taste, though.' She turned
back to her son. 'The girl's ashamed of marrying you.
Aren't you worried?'

'Not a bit,' a wave of his fingers dismissed the matter.
'Are you going to see to the arrangements, Mother?'

'That's what I've come down for,' Mrs Manfred spoke
grandly. 'Just give me the time and venue and the use of
a telephone and I'll start on the organisation. You can
have the reception at Griffins. How big do you want it?'
She fitted a cigarette into a long holder and lit it, allow-
ing a trickle of smoke to escape down her nostrils.
'Don't confuse me with numbers, please. Just say
whether you want it restrained or downright vulgar.'

Jerome's long lips quirked into a smile. 'Downright
vulgar, Mother. That's the sort you do best, isn't it? But
there are to be no Pressmen at the reception. We can't
keep them from the church door, but the reception is
private.'

Kate continued to sit with her arms around Philip,
who was growing bolder now. His head was raised and
he was examining his grandmother closely. She let the
conversation go back and forth over her head while she
also studied Mrs Manfred more closely. The coat which
was tossed negligently over the back of a chair was mink
and the lady's tailored suit was an exquisite blend of
heather tweed in a mixture that gave the impression of
being mainly lavender-coloured. The blouse under the

beautifully cut jacket was of pure silk and her feet were shod in expensive-looking plain court shoes. She was wearing very little jewellery. Kate's eyes drifted down to Mrs Manfred's hands and stayed there. They were unexpected hands, rather large and workmanlike with closely trimmed nails, hands which looked as if they were used. There was nothing of the pink-tipped, soft-looking fingers she had expected. She found herself liking those hands. They looked kind. . . .

'And now,' Mrs Manfred broke in on her thoughts, 'show me what you're wearing.'

Kate rose and went wearily to the bedroom door and gestured at the pile of unopened boxes. 'That!' she said indifferently.

Jerome's mother had no scruples about opening other people's boxes. Fancy tape, cardboard and tissue paper went flying in all directions as she burrowed. At last she raised her head.

'Impossible!' She was quite indignant. 'It might have been all right for a creepy little affair in a register office or even in the little church around the corner; if you were getting married at nine o'clock in the morning with just two witnesses and a taxi standing outside to take you straight to the airport, but it won't do for what Jerome has in mind. You'll cause more comment than either of you wish for, and it certainly won't do for a reception at Griffins. Not the sort of reception Jerome has asked for. You heard him—"Vulgar", that's what he said. We'll have to start all over again.' The thought seemed to please her and there was an excited sparkle in her blue eyes. 'I shall stay here with you. Jerome,' she waved a hand, dismissing all thoughts of him, 'Jerome can move into an hotel for the rest of the week. We'll get on better without him, anyway.'

One thing and one thing only saved the rest of the

week from being utterly unbearable. Kate found that her mother-in-law-to-be had no intention of going out to shop. She sat in the apartment, like a well corseted blonde spider; she comandeered the telephone and with an impressive arrogance, very like her son's, she lured the shops to her, not the whole shop but just those departments which interested her, and Kate had her own private mannequin parade of model wedding gowns which, she was assured, were definitely of the 'one off' variety, together with bridal veils and going-away clothes.

But even under these near utopian conditions, it all left her cold. Mrs Manfred, she recalled, had laughed at Shirley, and now that she had met her, she wasn't a bit surprised. Mrs Manfred seemed to laugh at everything; she was laughing now at the idea of a honeymoon for three.

'The boy won't enjoy it,' between her chuckles and bellows of mirth she was forthright. 'Too much travelling, all that foreign food, the change in climate; half the time he'll be tired to death and the other half he'll have an upset tum! Leave him with me.'

Kate shook her head firmly. 'I promised Shirley!'

Mrs Manfred looked her surprise. 'Shirley wasn't averse to leaving him with me before!' She sounded indignant. 'It was only that last time, when they were off to Crete. Theo had dismissed the nanny, you know; he said it was an economy measure, but I believe he couldn't stand the woman. A positive dragon of a female! Would you believe, she banned Theo from the nursery—said he was spoiling the child! I have to smile when I think about it, Theo practising economy! He always seemed so young to me, but I admit, after Philip was born Theo matured very quickly. Even Jerome noticed how responsible his brother had become.'

Kate nodded; there was nothing she could say. She had grieved for Shirley, and no matter what her opinion was of Shirley's young husband, he had been this woman's son and she had loved him. Mrs Manfred's grief would be as great, if not greater than her own.

'I thought they were taking the boy with them, he and Shirley.' Jerome's mother was almost thinking aloud. 'I didn't know they'd left him with you, I didn't even know that you existed. I thought . . .' her face went stiff with bitter memory, 'I thought he was in the car with them and when the police told us, "No survivors"——' She stopped swiftly and after a second or so rearranged her face into its hitherto pleasant expression. 'Now, what about flowers?' Calmly she changed the subject. 'I don't think one of those Victorian posy things is quite you, do you agree? You can carry off something much more splendid. Cream and gold, I think, with a hint of bronzy red. . . .'

With Jerome banished to an hotel, the sleeping arrangements in the apartment had been rearranged. Mrs Manfred now occupied the bed which had been Kate's and, leaving Philip and his puppy undisturbed, Kate had moved on to the couch to sleep. She had thought there might have been some objection to a dog on Philip's bed, but Jerome's mother had laughed at that as well.

'A golden Labrador, that's a good dog for a boy. There's something about a boy and a dog, they seem to go together, don't you think? But,' Mrs Manfred's eyes had twinkled, 'the dog's going to grow faster than Philip, so the sooner he learns not to sleep on the bed, the better. Not yet, of course, Philip needs the company and reassurance. I'll take the dog while you're away if you like.'

'You don't mind?' Kate felt surprise, although she

couldn't think why.

'Not in the least. I've an old terrier bitch who's feeling her age, and the pup will put new life into her. She's always been a good mother, but she's too old for breeding now and she trails round, trying to steal pups from the younger bitches. A bit like me!' Jerome's mother smiled ruefully and then became brisk. 'Nearly ten o'clock—off to bed with you, Kate, we've another busy day tomorrow. Finish that cup of tea while I check my list to see what's left to do. . . .'

Kate was drooping in her chair. They were both exhausted, she thought, and for the first time she noticed the lines of weariness around Mrs Manfred's mouth and eyes. Despite her prejudice against Jerome's mother, she was forced to admit that they got on very well together, and this was puzzling her. She should have been hating her, but it was quite impossible for her to hate Jerome's mother. She uttered the thought aloud and was surprised when that lady laughed uproariously.

'Of course you can't hate me, why should you? You're a nice, sensible, well balanced girl. I doubt if you could really hate anybody, and in any case, why me? Because your stepsister and I didn't always see eye to eye? There's nothing unusual in that, a great many daughters-in-law don't have a lot of love for their husbands' mothers. A man will treat his mother-in-law with affection, but a girl always seems to think that her husband's mother is trying to get the boy back, repossess the man-child. Ridiculous!' She chuckled. 'Shirley thought I was indelicate, did you know? Because I call a spade a spade. It comes of being brought up in the country. We had puppies and kittens instead of dolls, and ponies in place of bicycles. There was no nonsense about gooseberry bushes and what the fairies brought, or what the local midwife had in her little black bag!' She turned to Kate, her face a picture of distress. 'Your sister Shirley—I never could understand her, everything had to be wrapped up in cotton wool. We didn't get on at all. I wouldn't have minded so much, but. . . .' Kate never learned what Mrs Manfred wouldn't have minded because at that moment the outer door of the apartment was flung open and then slammed violently and a small dark-haired girl with black, passionate eyes erupted into the kitchen.

Mrs Manfred regarded the newcomer glacially. 'Estelle,' she said with no trace of surprise in her voice. 'Have you come to make a scene?' She turned to Kate. 'This is Estelle Rivers, Kate, a family friend. Estelle, Kate Forrest, who's marrying Jerome.'

Estelle quivered visibly. 'She can't marry Jerome!' The words came out shrill and fierce. 'Jerome's mine, he's always been mine! What's the matter, is she in the family way?'

Kate found her voice. 'No, I'm not!' she snapped.

Estelle ignored the interruption. 'Because if she is, Jerome had better make certain first that it's his. It's no use relying on the word of this little tramp. Where is Jerome? I must see him! I *have* to see him. He can't do this to me!'

'Don't be silly.' Mrs Manfred was brisk. 'I know you must be disappointed, but it's no use your coming down here in one of your famous rages. Jerome goes his own way, you know that, and your storms won't affect him one little bit.'

'Yes, they will!' Estelle hissed. 'I've been all day finding out about Kate Forrest, and when I've seen Jerome there won't be any wedding, I can promise you that!'

'Good!' Kate jumped to her feet. 'Then I'm off.'

'See?' Estelle almost shrieked in her triumph. 'She knows! She knows what I've discovered and she's wise enough to know when the game's up. Let her go.'

'Certainly not!' Mrs Manfred caught at Kate's skirt and jerked it. 'Sit down, Kate, and you sit down as well, Estelle—and for heaven's sake stop yelling. There's a child asleep in the room next door.'

'Another little bastard?' Estelle scowled her distaste, but she kept her voice down.

Mrs Manfred became almost arctic. 'No, it is not.' She was precise and over-polite. 'It's Philip. Kate's been looking after him since the accident. Now let's get a few things straight,' she raised a hand to quell the girl's next outburst. 'What exactly have you been "finding out"? And don't go into one of your ridiculous fantasies, they're usually too absurd for words, and I warn you, I shan't believe a word you say.'

'It's not a fantasy. The woman's been a model!' Estelle quivered with outrage.

'And that makes me unfit for human consumption?' Kate grabbed hold of her temper and hung on to that control grimly.

'Jerome knows what he wants.' His mother was bland but outspoken. 'If he wants to marry a model, that's his business. Personally, I think he's made a good choice, although he's taken long enough about it, and why should I object? I'm not marrying Kate, so it's nothing to do with me or with anybody except Jerome. When I saw him last he seemed quite satisfied—and why shouldn't he be?'

'She must be blackmailing him into it,' Estelle muttered fiercely, and at this reversal of the roles of blackmailer and victim, Kate burst into laughter which was almost hysterical.

'Stop that!' Mrs Manfred's voice was sharp. 'I didn't think you'd behave in that way, Kate. Didn't I say that you were sensible and well balanced? Now, Estelle, go back to your hotel or wherever it is you're staying, and if you feel you must kill yourself before morning, do it discreetly and without making too much mess. You know I hate blood. I don't think it's much use your waiting for Jerome, he may not be back.'

'He's sleeping with her, isn't he? He's bound to be back.' Estelle was truculent. 'I'll wait for him.' She then turned to Kate, appearing to notice her for the first time. 'Jerome gets these spasms, you know. I'm quite used to them. He sees some woman he just has to have and he sets off in pursuit. It never lasts more than six months and then he comes back to me.'

'Good!' Kate was acid. 'Then you'll only have to wait out the next six months, won't you?' She put down her cup with a distinct thump. 'I'm going to bed,' she informed her mother-in-law-to-be. 'As you said, tomorrow's another busy day, and I must get some sleep.' As she drew a bath and slipped out of her clothes, she thought about the little scene and shuddered. One point about it had cleared up a mystery, though. Kate knew now why Shirley had hated her mother-in-law. Mrs Manfred was outspoken and sharp and she had made it abundantly clear that she had little time for rages and sulks. Kate's mouth curved in a faint smile as she recalled the remark about Estelle killing herself. Shirley wouldn't have appreciated a remark like that! And yet Mrs Manfred apparently said that sort of thing frequently, judging by the way the volatile Estelle had ignored it. Shirley also had been given to spurts of temper and was capable of sulking for days on end until she finally got her own way. She wouldn't ever have got her own way with Jerome's mother.

Mrs Manfred had gone to bed and Kate was just making herself comfortable on the couch after hearing Estelle's staccato heel-taps receding down the hall and the slam of the front door of the apartment which meant that the girl had decided not to wait any longer. She looked up to find Jerome had come in. Without leave, he sat on the couch and leaned over her.

'Tired, Kate?'

'Very!' She glared back at him. 'We've sustained a visit from your best girl-friend. You'd better call this wedding off!'

'Oh no, the wedding will go ahead as planned, that was our bargain.'

'Estelle seems to think she has a prior claim.' She struggled with the blankets, tugging at them and trying to make herself more comfortable. 'She also thinks that I'm blackmailing you into marriage, which is the biggest joke of the century if it wasn't so damn tragic! She did offer one ray of hope, though, she told me that these little affairs of yours rarely last more than six months, so I told her to wait it out. I hope she does, and I hope she gets you. She has a perverted taste in men and she deserves you. You deserve her,' she added thoughtfully. 'She's quite impossible!'

Long fingers pushed the strap of her nightgown from her shoulder and Jerome lowered his head to nuzzle into the curve of her neck. Kate held herself rigid, hoping that he would not notice her fearful trembling or the frantic beat of her heart, but of course he did. His hand lay quietly on the softness of her breast, sounding the quickened heartbeat.

'None of this will affect the outcome, Kate. On Saturday you'll be Mrs Jerome Manfred.' Quiet, steady fingers slid the strap back into place and with no change of expression he rose and stood looking down at her. 'And while we're on the subject, Kate, don't allow your friend Gerald to rescue you. If you do that, I'll destroy him.' He said it quietly enough, almost conversationally, but there was a smooth menace below the words and she shuddered. 'Don't even think of him,' he smiled down into her frightened eyes. 'Ours will be a perfectly normal marriage and there'll be no room for thoughts of another man in our bed.'

She turned over so that she couldn't see him and buried her face in the pillow, stuffing her fingers in her ears to shut out his hateful, mocking voice, and she lay like that for a long time. When she at last turned, the room was in darkness and he had gone.

In the silent darkness she lay for a long time, wide awake, while she tried to sort out this crazy affair in the light of what little new knowledge she had gained that evening. Jerome, she eventually decided, was an economical man who liked killing as many birds with one stone as possible. Philip was one bird and the passionate Estelle was, evidently, another. It had to be that way. Nothing else made any sense. Estelle was pushing him.

So this was the famous Jerome Manfred! Hiding from one woman behind another. Kate's lips thinned and she whispered aloud in the darkness, 'Oh no, you're not hiding behind me!' If Estelle wanted him, she could have him and good luck to her! She was welcome to him, and as soon as this ridiculous 'honeymoon' was over she, Kate, would make certain that the girl had every chance to get her heart's desire. With a little cunning, it should be possible to land him in a nasty, sticky mess with the passionate Estelle! A small smile of unholy glee curved her mouth. It was dirty fighting—but then that was how he fought, and she *had* warned him!

CHAPTER FIVE

KATE survived the wedding. This was, in a way a great disappointment to her, since when she had woken on Saturday morning it had been with a chill hopelessness and a definite feeling that this wasn't happening to her, and if by some strange chance she wasn't dreaming, then something would have to happen to stop it. Common sense told her that, short of a tidal wave, an earthquake or a second Great Fire of London, nothing was going to stop this wedding taking place, and she momentarily regretted her distaste for alcohol. It would have been so much nicer if she could have sallied forth in a haze of alcoholic oblivion.

Mrs Manfred's cheerful 'Good morning' as she entered the bedroom with a breakfast tray sounded more like the knell of doom, and Kate regarded the contents of the tray with distaste. The toast looked greasy and the boiled egg was positively obscene. It wasn't, she knew that. It was just her jaundiced eye and her wish to die this very minute that was doing this to her. The tea was hot and refreshing, though, and she drank two cups full, holding the cup in both her nerveless hands to prevent herself from dropping it.

After a hurried shower, where the hot water felt as though it had come direct from the refrigerator, she went back to the bedroom to dress and Jerome's mother came bustling in, ready to help. Kate stood like a dressmaker's dummy while the white silk shift was pulled over her head and smoothed down over her waist and hips. Mrs Manfred had changed her mind about the white satin and lace and had settled for a gown in white velvet, cut on mediaeval lines with a low square neckline and wide hanging sleeves. This was put on over the silk thing and while Jerome's mother did up the countless little buttons which went all down the back of the fitted bodice, Kate looked at herself in the mirror and decided that for the sake of her own morale she would have to use a blusher on top of a creamy foundation. She could not allow herself to be seen looking like a whitewashed wall! She wasn't going to give Jerome the satisfaction of knowing that she was scared stiff!

Mrs Jerome sat her down at the dressing table and put the finishing touches to her face. She did it in a very professional way, and at Kate's look of wonder, she explained:

'I always wanted to act—the theatre—but of course it wasn't allowed. So when, much later, I had an opportunity to join an amateur dramatic society, I jumped at it. It was then I discovered that I couldn't act! So I contented myself with being useful, I've the right manner for direction and I do the make-up. I think I'm quite good at it.' She surveyed Kate's face intently. 'Don't you?'

'You're wonderful!' Kate looked at the healthy-looking face in the mirror and forced a smile.

Mrs Manfred had found somebody to give the bride away and Kate went down the aisle on the arm of an old gentleman with a very red face, very white hair and a military bearing. 'Slow march, my dear,' he whispered as he slowed her hurried pace, and through her veil she caught glimpses of a church full of people.

She made her responses in a barely audible voice. In the vestry, she signed her name with a shaking hand and was vaguely surprised that her signature was quite legible. Jerome's kiss had been cool and contained, but the hand that held hers held it firmly so that, when they emerged into the daylight and the flash of photographers' bulbs, she was even grateful for it.

At the reception, she fixed a bright smile on her face and kept it there. Everybody seemed excited and happy and she stood among them, isolated from them by the shell of cold misery which surrounded her. People kept coming up to her, shaking her hand or kissing her cheek, but they weren't real, not to her. Nothing was except the dark-clad man beside her. He said very little and looked as expressionless as a Buddha, yet she felt he was filled with satisfaction. Let him be satisfied! And she vowed grimly that it would be a shortlived satisfaction. She kept the sticky smile on her face while she decided that the new Mrs Jerome Manfred was going to be the most awkward and uncomfortable wife in the whole wide world. She saw Philip, clinging to his grandmother's hand and obviously enjoying himself, and she saw all the other empty, smiling faces. She hated them, every one of them, and wanted to scream at them to go away and stop being so damned happy.

By three o'clock in the afternoon her smile had become so rigid that she feared her face would crack, and she was vaguely grateful when Jerome took her arm firmly and announced that they were leaving. Kate had eaten nothing and washed it down with several glasses of champagne so that she was feeling dizzy and light-headed. She wished she had the courage to shake off that proprietorial hand and stalk out by herself, but the room was going round and the floor beneath her feet didn't feel very steady. Somebody wanted her flowers and she flung them from her with a feeling of relief, not even looking to see who had caught them.

Back in the apartment, she tore her way out of the white velvet and kicked the lovely dress half under the bed when it lay around her ankles. Her hair would do,

she decided; she had taken great pains with it that
morning and it still looked smooth. She patted a few
stray curls away from the nape of her neck and went
into the bathroom to wash away Jerome's mother's
work on her face before she touched it up again with a
fresh layer of foundation and dusted powder over it.
Her hand shook slightly as she tried to apply a little
lipstick, but she steadied her elbow on the top of the
dressing table and achieved quite a credible result before
she squirmed her way into the cream wool dress which
Mrs Manfred had decided would do after all for a going-
away outfit, and she tugged irritably at the zip. It
jammed and she found herself weeping with rage, frus-
tration and something like fear. Jerome chose this
moment to enter the bedroom, and she glared at his
reflection as he stood behind her.

'I'm dressing,' she said icily.

'And I am now your husband!' he said unconcernedly,
and his hand went out, unjammed the zip and pulled it
up. Kate felt his fingers against her back and again at
the nape of her neck as he fastened the minute hook
and eye at the top of the zip, and she shivered involun-
tarily. Then she pulled herself together and tried for a
little calm and common sense.

'Is Philip ready?'

'Mmm.' He was mocking her and she refused to look
up into his face. 'My mother resisted the temptation to
dress him in white velvet to match the bride, so he can
travel as he is. He's waiting for us in the car.'

Kate fastened on the subject of Philip and let it occupy
her mind to the exclusion of all else. She was living by
the hour, she reflected dully. One hour at a time and
concentrating on the 'now' so that she could push the
future away. 'I hope he hasn't been allowed to over-
eat,' she heard her own voice and it sounded strange, a

bit shrill. 'I don't want him being sick in your car.'

'We aren't going in the Ferrari.' Jerome sounded so matter-of-fact that she almost stopped shaking. 'Mother has lent us her chauffeur and her car. If Philip is sick in it, it will be her own fault for feeding him unsuitable things. Hurry now, please.'

Kate grabbed her handbag and went past him, thinking hard about Philip, Mrs Manfred's antique Rolls and her equally antique chauffeur. When the car turned off the main road and down into the small town of Staines, she was jerked out of her apathy.

'I thought . . . the airport . . . Heathrow. . . .'

'Not today.' Jerome slanted a glance down at her and then at the drowsy child on the seat beside her. 'Neither of you is fit to travel any farther today. Although Philip has spared us by not being sick, he's eaten too much, whereas you've eaten nothing. Tonight we shall stay in a nearby hotel. We can fly to Rome tomorrow morning when you've both had a rest. We shall stay there one night too and then we'll drive down to Calabria. It will be better for Philip.'

Kate had hardly expected this amount of consideration and her eyes widened. She would have liked to have waved it all away airily and insisted that they continue the journey as planned, but she felt too exhausted and hungry. That was a surprise to her, that she should feel hungry, but as she told herself grimly, the prisoner was always given a hearty meal before the execution. 'I'm hungry,' she announced, although it came out as a plaintive wail.

'Dinner has been ordered.'

That night she slept in a double bedroom with Philip while Jerome occupied the single room next door. There was a communicating door, but she locked it firmly. She lay in the darkness, listening to Philip's easy breathing, and felt half glad, half sorry. Was it a fate worse than death, or couldn't it be called that when it happened to a married woman? The silly thought brought a near-hysterical giggle to her throat. It wasn't happening tonight, though, and that pleased one half of her. The other half would have been glad to get it over. It was like being under sentence of death with the date of the execution fixed. She had been nearly prepared for it, she had had the hearty meal and she was in just the right frame of mind—numb! Now there had been a stay of execution and she had another twenty-four hours to get through and then try to recapture the numbness. Meanwhile she was here; alone, full of good food and tired to death.

She slept deeply and dreamlessly, so that when she woke, she gazed around at the unfamiliar room and for a moment wondered where she was. Then memory came rushing back and she drew her left hand from beneath the covers and looked at the heavy gold ring on her finger. Her eyes slid across to the other bed where Philip had been sleeping and she half rose in the bed as she realised that Philip was no longer there. She stopped being frightened only when the bedroom door opened and the little boy and Jerome came in quietly, or as quietly as Philip ever came into a room. He flung himself at her, scrambling to sit comfortably on her stomach.

'Jumbo jet!' he announced, and then, 'Fly!' His short arms stretched out on either side of his stout little body and he made the appropriate noises.

'I locked that door!' Kate glared at her husband.

'A pass key.' He looked unperturbed. 'Philip was awake, I could hear him, so I came and collected him. He's had a shower and he's dressed. If you hurry, we'll have time for breakfast.'

'Philip doesn't like showers,' she objected.

'He does now.' There was the ghost of a smile about Jerome's mouth. 'You've been too soft with him, Kate. He needs a firmer hand.'

'And now I suppose you're going to take over?' She was sarcastic.

'Mmm, when necessary—but stop wasting time. Get dressed and come to breakfast. I'll take Philip down now.'

'Thank you,' she said grudgingly, and deliberately waited until he had left the room before she threw back the covers and started to hunt through her cases for something to wear. The cream and coffee outfit belonged to yesterday, which hadn't been a 'good' day. Perhaps today would be better.

She entered the dining room a quarter of an hour later, neat and precise in a thin charcoal grey suit worn with a pale green silk blouse. There was a short leather jacket lying on top of her case in the bedroom, in case she should be cold, and the cream and coffee gear had been bundled to the bottom of her luggage. Kate felt quite cheerful this morning and wanted no reminders of what she now thought of as the worst day of her life.

Philip, who had finished his cereal and was now busy dipping toast soldiers into his boiled egg, spared her a glance.

'Fly with Uncle,' he was emphatic. 'Goodbye!'

Kate accepted the coffee which the waiter was proffering and glared at her husband for the second time that morning.

'You've been brainwashing him,' she scolded as she helped herself to cream and sugar and buttered a piece of toast lavishly.

The flight to Rome was boring; there was no delightful view of patchwork fields to look down upon, neither did Kate catch a glimpse of the sea. She saw only the topsides of clouds which looked so much like the undersides of clouds that she found difficulty in convincing herself that she was not upside down. Philip behaved himself beautifully, sitting on either her knee or Jerome's and beaming widely at the stewardesses and playing with a plastic model of an aeroplane while making the appropriate noises.

In the Rome hotel there was another stay of execution which thoroughly upset Kate. She had been feeling much better—and why shouldn't she? she asked herself. Nobody could live in a welter of gloom for ever, and two of her biggest gloom-makers had been eliminated. She no longer had to fear that the Manfreds would find her and Philip, they had already done so, and she need not fear that they would whip Philip away and she would never see him again, because that wasn't going to happen either. In fact, she had only one great trial to face; her mind shuddered away from it, and she wished she had the courage to invade Jerome's bedroom and say, 'Do it now and get it over!' But she did no such thing. She curled up on her comfortable mattress, between sheets which felt like silk, twitched a lace-trimmed pillow beneath her cheek and slept like a baby.

And now, she thought as she stepped stiffly from the car, here is Calabria, and she sought vainly for the blissful numbness which she had felt in the hotel near Staines. The house facing her was old—'primitive', Jerome had said, but it was lovely, a golden stone with all the corners worn smooth by weather and time and with a faded red pantiled roof with tremendous eaves which overhung the walls. The windows were tall and narrow and the upper ones had little wrought iron balconies which bulged outwards like cabriole legs, and the side walls of the house had been extended in a series of arches to surround a large square tiled courtyard.

And over everything was a sharp, sweet perfume that was in the air itself. Kate sniffed appreciatively and hung on grimly to Philip, who had spotted a fountain in the middle of the courtyard and wanted to throw himself into it.

Jerome noticed the sniff. 'Bergamot,' he explained. 'The sweet lime. It's the main crop in this area, used in perfume and tea among other things, and during the harvest, when the skins are being squeezed to extract the oil, you can smell nothing else. Come inside and meet Constantina, she'll look after you. Her English is limited, but you'll manage.'

Constantina took one look at Philip and ignored everything else. She clapped her hands to her kerchief-covered head in delight and yelled an incomprehensible sentence which ended with the word *bambino*, and Philip, who even at this early age could recognise a child-worshipper when he saw one, smiled fatly, nodded his dark curls and offered a kiss. Kate watched them go, the little plump old lady, her long black skirts swinging under her white apron, and the little boy skipping at her side. Constantina was chattering as if there was no to-morrow and Philip was basking in adulation.

Kate walked in through the door very slowly and made polite conversation. 'It's warmer here,' she ventured. 'Warmer than in England, I mean.'

Jerome matched her inanity. 'The average January temperature is fifty degrees Fahrenheit. It's warmer than that now and this side of Calabria is dryer than the side facing Sicily.'

'And the chief crop is bergamot,' Kate finished the geography lesson. 'Is there a bathroom?' She heard herself make the stiff, polite query and wished frantically that she could be normal and waspish as she followed him up the stairs and watched him put their cases in one room. The bed looked very large and quite modern, and she caught herself on the edge of hysterical laughter. What did it matter what the bed looked like?

'Yes, there is a bathroom.' Jerome was matter-of-fact. 'But that's where the primitive part comes in. There's no hot water system. The villa is not generally used except during the summer when I find a cold shower sufficient, but Constantina will toil around with jugs of hot water if you like.'

'Oh no!' she babbled. 'I wouldn't dream of asking. It's not too cold for a cold shower, in fact it will help me to wake up a bit. It's just that I feel a bit grubby and sticky after the journey.' At this point her tongue stuck to the roof of her mouth, she felt tears in her eyes and a painful lump in her throat. 'I can't,' she whispered, while her eyes slid to the bed.

'Welshing on our agreement, Kate?' He sounded exasperated. 'It's no more than I expected. Your face has worn a white martyred look since Saturday. I've given you enough time, surely, and so far I've not forced you into anything.'

'Yes, you have!' She flung the words at him. 'You would have taken Philip away from me.'

'Then we must hope you find Philip worth the—er—sacrifice.' He was unsympathetic as he abstracted clean clothes from a case and left her alone in their bedroom.

Within a short while Constantina was tapping at the door. With a very few English words, a few more Italian and a lot of mime, she made Kate understand that Philip had eaten, drunk, been bathed and was now in his bed and sleeping like an angel; that there was a meal ready for the Signor and Signora and that it was all to be eaten, and furthermore, that she, Constantina, was happy! Jerome came in at the end of the monologue and it was all repeated to him, but without the English

words or the mime, just a swift torrent of Italian. He
smiled at the little woman as she bustled out.

'Did you get all that?' he enquired lazily.

'Most of it.' Kate sat down wearily on the bed.
'Philip's been bathed, fed and put to bed where he's
now sleeping, we're to eat all our dinner and
Constantina is happy.'

'But my wife is not. Hmm?' He was harsh. 'Where's
your pride, Kate? To be beaten by only the thought of a
bridal night! Don't you think you're being excessively
modest? After all, you're twenty-six years old and few
women of your age are expected to have led a nunlike
existence. I thought better of you than this. Come here.'

Kate sat unmoving except to put up a hand to sweep
her hair away from her forehead. So that was what he
thought of her! Dully she wondered what he would say
if she told him that this would be the first time for her.
She stole a look at the dark, harsh, cynical face and
decided to say nothing. He would probably tell her to
pull the other one, it had bells on it!

'Come here!' Jerome repeated the command more
sharply and she rose to her feet and crossed the room to
where he was standing. A long finger tilted her chin.

'You have several smuts on your face and a few more
on your shirt. Your skirt is creased where Philip has
been sitting on your knee and your nose is shiny. Go
and tidy yourself, then we'll have dinner and talk. You'll
feel better when you've eaten.'

Past him, in the long pier-glass, Kate caught a glimpse
of herself and nearly died with shame. It was even worse
than he had said, and with a gasp of horror she grabbed
her toilet bag and fled to the bathroom.

Dinner was quite pleasant and under other circumstances, Kate would have enjoyed herself. The *peperonata*
was the best she had ever eaten, and she wished she had

more appetite to do it justice, and there was a delicious sweet of bottled cherries and whipped cream that tasted heavenly. At the end of the meal, as Jerome had said, she did feel much better. She dismissed the idea of asking him humbly to be gentle with her, she was not going to sue for quarter at this late stage, but she was able to stop halfway up the stairs and look back at him where he stood at the stairfoot, watching her.

'Rape is not a pretty word,' she told him severely.

Jerome was unmoved, as she knew he would be. 'I'm going to bed with my wife, Kate. It won't be rape!'

'Then you'll have to forgive my ignorance,' she snapped back at him, 'if I don't notice the difference.'

Later, lying rigid and praying for some sort of unconsciousness, she felt him slide between the sheets, then there was a hard arm about her and firm hands which deliberately divested her of her nightgown. She gasped with outrage and started to struggle, but a cool mouth found hers, cutting off the blistering words on her tongue while his hands moved about her. At first they only held her arms to her sides while his mouth blazed a trail from her forehead down to her breasts, then they began to caress insidiously so that after a while she stopped struggling and gave herself up with a moan of despair. Almost without consciousness on her part, she found her hands tangled in the crisp hair at the back of his head and she was holding him to her while his mouth slid over the slender curves of her body, sending a flame leaping through her. And then there was only a savage need which demanded satisfaction, a sharp, sweet pain, a wild surge of something like victory and a deep contentment.

She woke to a pale grey light at the window and lay watching as it deepened to lemon. When she tried to move, the arm about her tightened, denying her even that small liberty. She turned her head away from Jerome and gazed at the white, roughly plastered wall with a chill hopelessness.

No, it hadn't been rape! But the wildness of the night was now gone and morning had reduced everything to a shameful memory. That she should have behaved in such a way—she couldn't even bear to think of the word 'abandoned'. She closed her eyes, fighting back tears, and then common sense took over. Self-disgust? Yes, she could feel that, it was allowable, but shame? No! She had done nothing for which she need feel shame. She had not forced Jerome into marriage, neither had she forced herself upon him. She was the injured party, and as she winced as she moved, she thought grimly that she would have the bruises to prove it. She had pitted her abysmal ignorance and inexperience against an expert, and she had lost. She need feel neither shame nor embarrassment.

She wriggled around until she could peer over the side of the bed in a search for her nightgown. The arm tightened and pulled her back, turning her to face him.

'Not rape, Kate!'

'No.' She raised her eyes and kept them quiet and steady on his. 'I'm not experienced enough to give it a name. It was something purely animal, I suppose. I'm not ashamed of myself, but I am filled with self-disgust, and I think I shall never forgive you for it—for making me behave like an animal, I mean. I disliked you and distrusted you before and I came as near to hating you as it was possible for me to hate anybody. Now, I *do* hate you. Not for what you've done to me, but for what you made me do. And don't bother telling me that it's all my own fault, I know that already.' Her mouth grew wry. 'But I wasn't much of an opponent, was I? A green girl up against an expert!' She made a face. 'I didn't stand a chance!'

'Correct.' He pulled her down against him so that she felt the hardness of his thigh against her and she held her breath as traitorous warmth started to steal through her body. She heard him laugh softly, a nasty, triumphant laugh. 'A very green girl—a virgin! I hadn't expected that; I'd begun to think they were an extinct species, but you can't fight an expert, Kate, so why try?'

'I must!' she said desperately even as she felt herself weakening. 'Even if I don't stand a chance, even though I know I'll lose every time, I still have to fight.'

'Why?' His hand slid down to the curve of her body to her hip, tightened on the delicate bone and pulled her hard against him.

Despite the shivers running over her body, from some unknown depths she dredged up a little sarcasm. 'Call it my nuisance value. I'm a fighter by nature.'

'Why bother?' he murmured against her mouth, his body a warm, heavy weight on hers. 'Learn a few simple rules, Kate,' it was not much more than a whisper, 'the first being that no man wants a practical discussion when he's giving pleasure to a woman.'

When she next woke, it was broad daylight, the sun was high and Philip was bouncing on her chest. 'Sea,' he was chanting. 'Swim! Fiss!'

'Fish!' she corrected him automatically while she endeavoured to draw the covers over her bare shoulders.

'Fiss,' he agreed amiably before he was removed from the bed. Jerome was behind him, looking rather piratical in a dark jersey and slacks. Kate glowered at him with what she hoped was a glacial eye and slid farther down in the bed.

'Here on the coast, fish is nearly the staple diet. Constantina wants some, so we must go and catch it.'

His tone was severely practical.

'You don't require me for that,' she muttered. 'I've never caught fish in my life, I wouldn't know how to start.'

'You aren't required to catch fish,' he was reasonable. 'Your task will be to ensure that Philip doesn't fall overboard. I shall tie him to the mast of the boat and you will sit with him and keep him quiet. I shall do the fishing.' His glance flicked over her in a most embarrassing way and he tucked Philip under one arm and went off downstairs, leaving Kate prey to a number of emotions which she had never known she possessed.

The cold shower restored her to nearly normal and she went down the stairs in pale blue jeans and a white pullover, her feet making no sound in soft sneakers.

'Charming and practical,' Jerome approved her clothes as she helped herself to coffee. 'May I?' He passed her another cup and she busied herself pouring it while Constantina pattered in and out in flat sandals which made slapping noises on the tiles of the floor. Despite her resolution, Kate felt embarrassment—or was it that? Wasn't it more like envy? Yes, she decided, it was much more like envy. She wished she could behave as he did, as if nothing had happened—but that's what experience does for you, she told herself wryly, and sat drinking coffee while she longed for the day when she also would have sufficient experience to be able to sit calmly, with no thought of the night before, just an ability to look forward to the day ahead. She bit into a warm roll and ventured some polite conversation. Two words only, they came out a bit jerkily, but at least she was trying.

'What fish?'

'Nothing you would know.' There was no embarrassment in him as he passed his coffee cup to be refilled.

'There's no cod or haddock here.' His gaze slid past her to the window. 'I recommend that we leave soon,' and at her look of surprise, he continued smoothly, 'before our nephew flings himself into the fountain.'

The 'honeymoon' lasted ten days, ten days during which Kate learned a lot. She learned not to be embarrassed; it was difficult anyway when Jerome treated everything as being perfectly normal, perfectly ordinary. He seemed well satisfied with his strange bargain and Kate was quiet and submissive; at least she was as submissive as it was in her nature to be. She was living for the day when she would be back in England and could do something. They spent long days in the quite warm sunshine, sitting in the courtyard reading or walking along the rough grey-white roads with Philip mounted on a tiny donkey. Several times Kate tried to start a really serious conversation with Jerome, a conversation which would run on the lines that now he knew she wasn't a promiscuous type of woman, now he knew that she was in all respects a decent person who could be trusted to care for a child properly ... but her faltering tongue stilled under his mocking gaze and the hot blood rose in her cheeks, so the conversation never took place.

The evenings were the worst part, after Philip had gone to bed, although she had discovered that a couple of glasses of wine with dinner gave her quite a euphoric feeling and enabled her to play cards for pence with a reckless abandon. But Jerome had stopped that.

'I do not want a drunken woman in my bed,' and he had removed the wine bottle from her fingers. That showed how insensitive he was, she glowered at him; once through the bedroom door the euphoria deserted her and she was stone cold sober. But it was as he had said, she reflected. This was a period of adjustment, and as they boarded the plane in Rome, she decided that she was not quite as well adjusted as she would have liked to be.

They didn't go to the apartment when they returned to London, instead the waiting limousine at the airport swept them to a small house in Kensington and it was there, in the tastefully furnished sitting-room, that Jerome showed his teeth.

'Tobias,' he had introduced her to the middle-aged, blunt-featured man who had driven the car. 'And this is Mrs Davies, his wife, who is your cook–housekeeper. There is a maid—Ellen, I think,' and he had smiled down at Mrs Davies in quite a kind way.

'That's right, sir,' the housekeeper had folded firm, hardworking hands. 'Ellen, our youngest. I think you'll find her satisfactory, madam.'

Kate murmured that she was sure she would and, sitting down, thankfully poured herself a cup of tea. It was the first tea she had drunk since they had left London over ten days ago and it tasted like nectar. She sighed with relief. She was not a particularly good traveller and Philip had been bored, irritable and aggravating on the last stage of the journey, so that it had seemed to go on for ever. When the door closed behind the housekeeper, Jerome seated himself, accepted a cup of tea and announced blandly that tomorrow morning she would be busy and she was therefore to keep it free.

'Learning the geography of a gentleman's residence?' Kate was acid.

'No,' he remained bland. 'Interviewing nurses.'

'Nurses?' She put her cup down very carefully. 'I don't need a nurse.'

'You may not, Kate, but Philip does. He's becoming thoroughly spoiled—and in any case, you won't have as much time to spare for him from now on.'

Kate's eyes glittered nastily. 'You're mistaken! All my

time is Philip's. He doesn't need a nurse, he has me.'

'No!' He put down his cup and rose to his feet, seeming to tower over her. 'When it's convenient, we're leaving for Derbyshire where we will stay with my mother for a week or so, and when we return to London there'll be a certain amount of entertaining. We shall receive invitations to dinner and things like that, and we can't refuse them all. In return, people will expect to be invited here. Furthermore, the house is not yet completely furnished or finished, there are still several rooms which have to be decorated. You're going to be busy, therefore there will be a nurse for Philip.'

'I prefer to look after Philip myself,' she told him truculently. 'You don't understand. What should I do with my time otherwise? I wasn't brought up to a life of leisure nor to be idle. As for the entertainment part of it, I've never done any and I don't think I'd be any good at it. What's more, I don't want to!'

'You ask what you will do with your time?' He raised an eyebrow. 'What do women ever do with their time? Aren't there frequent visits to shops and dressmakers, then there's the hairdresser and coffee mornings, bridge afternoons and things like that. You'll have to superintend the household, although you can safely leave the cooking and day-to-day running to Mrs Davies. As for your never having done much entertaining, we'll accept a few invitations first, so that you can see how it's done and then you can experiment. You'll soon pick it up, you're a clever girl, not a fool. So there *will* be a nurse for Philip, either of your choosing or mine.' Hard fingers came under her chin, forcing her face up and holding it firmly so that she could not escape without an undignified struggle. 'You'll make an excellent hostess, Kate,' he murmured.

She stared into his grey eyes and quite suddenly she

was obsessed with a desire to please him, but she dismissed it. She was a fool and becoming weak!

'Coffee mornings would remind me of morning breaks at school, in the staff room, and I never cared for them. Nor can I play bridge, I'm not nearly clever enough. I'd rather look after Philip.'

'No,' he shook his head. 'Philip must learn that he can't have all your time. He must learn to share you, otherwise there'll be trouble when we have children of our own.'

'You envisage that?' Shock made her voice shake.

'Of course.' He was enigmatic again. 'I should think it's inevitable. Kindly oblige me by not doing anything to stop it.'

Mrs Davies came in at that moment to remove the tea tray and Kate gave her husband a smile of saccharine sweetness for her benefit.

CHAPTER SIX

KATE stirred drowsily and blinked against the morning light. It took her several seconds to orientate herself, and then she recalled where she was, in the Kensington house. She turned over sleepily, aware now, as she always was aware, of the arm closely about her and the warm body lying close to her in the bed. Her movement caused the arm to tighten and she felt Jerome stir beside her.

'Still hate me, Kate?' From the tone of the words it seemed that he didn't care whether she did or not, but all the same, she nodded and pulled the quilt up over her shoulders to cover her nakedness. This amused Jerome. 'You're such a private person, my dear, and you make it so obvious that I can't resist invading that privacy, but not this morning. I've a board meeting at ten and a very heavy day. Expect me at six—meanwhile, choose a good nurse.' He slid out of bed and with a slap at the hump which was her rear, went off to the bathroom.

And she *did* hate him, Kate told herself so all through her shower and dressing, and deliberately ignored the small inner voice which said, 'Nonsense, no such thing! You're getting quite used to him, and nobody can possibly hate someone they're getting used to!' There was a police theory, she remembered, that, given time, a rapport grew between captor and captive, and she wondered if a rapport was growing between Jerome and herself, then dismissed the idea as ridiculous. If anything was growing it was her sense of outrage and the irritating lack of privacy.

She inspected herself carefully in the mirror to see that she conformed with the image of Kate Forrest who was going to bore him to death, and was quite pleased with what she saw. A severely straight, dark skirt, a very plain shirt with a mannish collar and cuffs and nice, sensible shoes. She spared a moment to tighten her hair back a little and went off downstairs to the tiny breakfast room to catch Jerome before he left. At the door she drew a deep breath, straightened her back and marched in, her shoulders squared and determination in every line of her body.

'After lunch, when I've seen this nurse you're so insistent upon, I'm going to see Helen!' Her eyes sparked, daring him to say 'no'. She was not going to grovel for permission, she was giving him a plain statement of intent!

'Mmm.' He folded the newspaper he was reading and passed her his empty coffee cup for refilling. 'Why the belligerence?'

Carefully she poured him the coffee and passed it before answering. 'I don't know the rules,' she pointed out sarcastically. 'For all I know, you might have a complex about impecunious artists of the hardworking loyal type. You mightn't think them the right sort of company for me to keep. Perhaps it would be a good idea if you had one of your secretaries type out a list of "Do's and Don't's". I could pin it to the bedroom wall and consult it every morning.'

'The restrictions are very few.' Jerome stirred his coffee and held her gaze. 'They operate for your safety and wellbeing, also Philip's, and for my peace of mind as well. You will never take the boy out unless either the nurse or Tobias is with you, and if you want to go anywhere alone, Tobias will drive you, wait for you and bring you back.'

'How nice!' A bitter kind of honey dripped from her tongue. 'I'm so glad you've told me. So the nurse is going to double up as a wardress, is she? I must remember to choose one who looks the part. Have you any particular qualifications in mind? Do you demand a judo black belt or would the first part of a course in karate be good enough?'

Jerome sighed wearily at her. 'Don't be childish, Kate! It doesn't become you. There's a perfectly good reason for most things I do. I'm a wealthy man, a member of a wealthy family, and even here in London kidnapping is not unheard-of.'

Just for a very short moment she felt like a badly behaved schoolgirl, but then she gave a mental snort. Jerome might possibly be concerned for Philip, but for herself, she doubted if his concern covered anything more than his bank balance; it was not for her, not personally. While these thoughts were running through her head, he had pushed back his chair, risen to his feet and come to stand behind her, his hand on her shoulder.

'One other restriction, Kate. No contact with Gerald Twyford, please. I think I explained once before what would happen if you made a move in that direction, and I'm sure you remember. Apart from these few small things, you may do what you please, within reason.'

'Then I'll certainly go to see Helen this afternoon,' she muttered, adding as an afterthought, 'I should have invited her to the wedding.'

Jerome's hands were heavy on her shoulders and they gave her a little shake. 'I thought there was something withdrawn about you the day we were married.' He sounded amused. 'We did invite Helen and she came, didn't you notice? She gave us a rather charming charcoal sketch of you and Philip.'

Delight robbed her voice of its former acidity. 'Did she? How lovely. I must see that!'

'Then open you eyes, my dear wife. It's in the sitting-room, over the fireplace—and while we're on the subject of wedding presents, there's a list on the desk in the study. You'd better make a start on the "thank you" letters.'

'But I haven't seen any of them,' she protested. 'How can I thank people for things I've not even looked at?'

'Quite simply.' His hands left her shoulders and slid down to her waist, pulling her up and turning her to face him. 'You say that whatever it is is very lovely or very useful and that we'll treasure it for the rest of our lives.' He was pulling her closer and Kate was holding herself rigid as she tried to think of something to distract him.

'There was a girl on the stairs as I came down, she had a vacuum cleaner.'

'That will be Mrs Davies's "our Ellen". One of the unfortunates—I believe they're known as "educationally subnormal". Make allowances for her, please, we don't want to lose the Davieses. Tobias knows his job and Mrs Davies is a very good cook.'

Kate glared at him. 'How dare you! To suggest that I would. . . . I've been a teacher, remember? I wouldn't penalise a child or her parents for something that wasn't their fault. Most of the E.S.N.s are very nice anyway, I never found them much trouble at all. It's the intelligent ones that cause most of the bother.'

'Then you must get that point over to Mrs Davies.' Jerome was looking as if it was all her fault. 'She'll be worrying until you put her mind at rest—and by the way, I've told her to call you Mrs Jerome when she's not saying madam; that way, she won't muddle you up with my mother.' He inspected her face closely and looked relieved. 'Not too much make-up. I think I can risk it,' and he bent his head and kissed her very thoroughly before he went quietly out, closing the door behind him.

When he had gone Kate sat morosely, leaving the coffee to cool in her cup. She didn't understand—oh, not about his parting kiss, that had just been Jerome being aggravating, demonstrating that he could do as he liked when he liked; she was becoming used to that. No, it was herself she couldn't understand. If she could only have talked it out—but for that she needed somebody totally remote from the mess she was in, somebody who could look at it from the outside and offer words of comfort and wisdom. She grinned to herself ruefully. There wasn't anybody!

Whoever she spoke to would have to be a complete stranger, otherwise they might be biassed one way or the other, and she couldn't imagine herself pouring out her heart to a complete stranger. The only thing for her to do was to get on with the mundane business of living, even though it was proving very difficult to live with herself, her new self which Jerome had created. This new, wanton Kate who dissolved into a passionate puddle and who accepted his lovemaking with an uninhibited response that appalled her!

There was one little ray of sunshine in the gloom. At least now Jerome couldn't have such a bad opinion of her. He couldn't accuse her, as he had implied before, of being promiscuous. He knew better now, and he had admitted it. Kate worried the problem a bit more and finally gave up in despair. Whichever way she looked at it, the needle was pointing to 'Stormy and Unsettled'. Perhaps she could concentrate on the good points? Philip was happy, that was one bright spot, and they were together; they no longer had to run and hide, and she had finished completely with Noelle Lowe. That other self no longer existed.

Her faint stirrings of relief were interrupted by the thought of the nurse. Philip would now have his nanny and she, Kate, would be gently but firmly pushed out of his life. As for Noelle, she wasn't really finished with her, was she? Not while Jerome had those negatives. She was back at the beginning again. She rose and, remembering, rushed back upstairs.

For convenience, Philip's cot had been placed in her dressing room last night and when she had come downstairs he had been sleeping quite heavily, but Philip was equipped with some sort of radar sense so that, no matter how heavily he might be asleep, he always woke when there was nobody within screaming distance. Then, he either tried to shake the cot to pieces or climb over the side. Both were disastrous and always ended up in tears.

Philip's radar was working beautifully this morning and Kate found him peering through the bars of the cot like a caged animal and uttering piercing yells of temper. Hastily she grabbed him and whisked him off to the bathroom, where he suffered her to wash several minute sections of his skin before demanding food. He didn't want to be dressed or cuddled, he wanted cornflakes. Kate sighed with exasperation as she struggled him into his clothing, and then had an idea whereby she could kill two birds with one stone. She hoisted her squirming nephew under one arm and made her way back to the kitchen, where she marched firmly in and dumped her wriggling burden on the tiled floor.

Kate put on her calm teacher's face as she felt the battery of two pairs of eyes assessing her. Both pairs, those of the housekeeper and 'our Ellen', were alight with curiosity and a lurking suspicion, but she ignored it as she had learned to ignore the same glint in the eyes of a new class of children.

'Good morning,' she smiled brightly. 'I'm afraid I've let the coffee get cold. Could I . . .?'

'You should have rung, madam.' Mrs Davies was severe.

'Mmm, but it wasn't worth it.' Kate gave her a pleasant smile. 'I only wanted one cup. May I have it here? I was feeling a bit chilly and your kitchen's so beautifully warm. No,' she added swiftly as she saw the housekeeper's mouth open to speak, 'don't turn up the heating. It's just me, I think. I haven't adjusted to the lower temperature yet and I'm still a bit tired, I expect.'

The coffee was very hot and Kate ladled in sugar and cream with a lavish hand while she pondered. By the time the cup was empty, she had decided on her course of action.

'Philip is washed and dressed and I'd like him to have his breakfast in here if possible,' she gestured at the tiled floor. 'Much better, don't you think? His eating habits are rather messy and until Nurse is installed and he can have his meals in the nursery. . . . Then, if you would allow Ellen to keep him amused while we have a quick look around the house and I interview the nurses—that is, if you can spare her . . .?'

'Indeed I can.' The housekeeper flushed with pleasure and beamed at her silent daughter while Kate felt relief. Jerome had said to put Mrs Davies's mind at rest about 'our Ellen' and she congratulated herself that she had done it quite diplomatically.

It was a very pleasant house, not over-large but elegant, and it had been recently restored or repaired. Kate noted that the bathing and toilet facilities were more than adequate. Three rooms remained undecorated and unfurnished, although they had been recently plastered, and the woodwork had been painted a dazzling white.

Two were guest rooms on the first floor and the other, a small drawing-room, on the ground floor and overlooking the garden.

Mrs Davies explained, 'We've only been here three days ourselves and Mrs Manfred said "First things first, get the nursery suite ready. There has to be a place for the boy and his nanny." Well, I suppose you can't expect a nurse to come unless there's somewhere ready for her! Mrs Manfred sent the other furniture down from Derbyshire—it was better here, she said, than collecting dust in her attics. Good stuff, it is, better than you can buy. The bedrooms and the drawing-room she left empty. She said she'd interfered enough and you'd want some part of it,' the housekeeper explained. 'That's what Mrs Manfred said.'

So, Kate breathed in deeply, she was once more obligated to Jerome's mother, and she didn't want to be under any more obligation to the Manfreds. She didn't consider Jerome's munificence in quite the same light—she was paying for that! But as for his mother, she wanted to be able to hate with a clear conscience. She would have liked to go to Jerome and tell him that she would choose her own housekeeper, if she had to have one, but she couldn't do that now, not to a woman like Mrs Davies who was struggling to keep an unfortunate daughter with her. In her pity for the housekeeper, she forgot her own problems for a while until she glanced at her watch and realised that she had only ten minutes before the applicants arrived for the nursing post. She walked back with the housekeeper to the kitchen and begged a cup of coffee. While she was drinking it, she remembered what Jerome had said about entertaining.

'How do you feel about it?' she asked, after she had explained. The housekeeper snorted as she unplugged the percolator.

'It won't be much, not unless Mr Jerome's changed a lot since he was young. He was never one for a lot of socialising. A quiet place, some nice music or a book, that's Mr Jerome. And,' she looked sideways at Kate, 'though I'm a good cook, I've not much time for these foreign kickshaws. Good plain English cooking, that's what I'm best at. Give me a nice joint or a good plump bird any time. There's nothing in these pasta and rice dishes but a lot of leftovers dressed up to look like something they're not.' She sniffed disparagingly. 'I'm not fashionable,' she concluded.

'Then we'll have to be unfashionable,' Kate smiled widely. 'We'll have what you're best at.'

Mrs Davies's voice followed her to the kitchen door. 'You'll please the men anyway. Men don't like bits!'

There were four nurses and not one of them was under forty-five years of age. Kate hid her surprise very well. Somehow she had been convinced that Jerome would have wanted young, nubile girls, but from what she gathered as she conducted the interviews, it had been the exact reverse. His instructions to the Agency had been quite explicit—a children's nurse, competent, reliable and past the first flush of youth.

With Philip in mind and trying to set aside her own prejudices, Kate chose the one who seemed to think that the little boy was of the first importance. The other three had demanded to see the accommodation first, so Kate found herself warming towards the one who did not enquire whether the bed had an orthopaedic mattress, whether there was a maid to attend to the nurse's wants and how much free time would be available. This one was the least starchy and had not been at all disturbed when Philip had greeted her with a mouthful of biscuit and had sprayed her all over with crumbs in the process.

Mrs Davies had sent 'our Ellen' along to the study with a tea tray, and Kate asked, 'When can you come?' as she poured tea with a steady hand and acted as though she interviewed staff every day of the week.

'Oh, at once, Mrs Manfred, if that's what you require.' The small, brisk woman nodded cheerfully, her round grey pork pie hat bouncing on her greying head. 'I live with my sister while I'm between jobs and I can easily fetch my few things in a taxi. When would you like me to come?'

Kate felt no hesitation. 'Today,' she said firmly, 'and as soon as possible—and there's no need for you to get a taxi. I'll send Tobias with you and he'll bring you and your luggage back.' And within an hour Miss Emily Hogg (such an unfortunate name, Mrs Manfred) was installed and Philip appeared to be more than satisfied. Kate felt a tug at her heartstrings at Philip's blithe acceptance of this replacement of herself, but of course, he was only a small boy, she excused his infidelity. He didn't understand. All the same, it hurt a bit to think that she could be so easily replaced.

Helen greeted her with a hoot of pleasure. 'How's it going?' she enquired practically after the first greetings and 'do you remembers' had been exchanged and they were sitting together in the big, untidy studio and drinking coffee from thick stoneware mugs.

'So-so.' Kate put a mental ban on her tongue and changed the subject. There were some things that couldn't be talked about, even with Helen. 'Thank you for the sketch. It's one of the nicest wedding presents I could have wished for. Jerome likes it too, he's already had it framed and it's hanging in the sitting-room. There's a load of other stuff as well, most of it's not been unpacked yet. I'm going to have writer's cramp doing the thank-you letters.'

'I'm honoured.' Helen looked very pleased. 'Hanging already, you say? Well, you never know! It might lead to a few commissions now you're mixing with the moneyed bracket. You don't look estatically happy, I must say.' Helen returned to the attack.

'I'm tired,' Kate admitted. 'It's been a hectic three weeks and I think I've lost track of time. The cottage seems a lifetime away.' Somehow the conversation was stilted and unnatural as if, in the space of three short weeks, she had grown away from Helen, but it wasn't that, of course. It was that she was having to think of everything before she said it; there were so many things, important things, she just couldn't talk about.

Helen watched the play of expression over Kate's mobile face and leaned back in her chair, thrusting her hands into the deep pockets of her paint-stained smock.

'Come on, love,' she coaxed. 'You've been sitting there looking martyred ever since you came in. It can't be as bad as that, surely? Tell Aunty Helen all about it and she'll advise you.'

'I can't do that,' Kate protested. 'Things are a bit upside down just at present and I'm still trying to work out which way up they ought to be.'

'Uncertainty!' Helen dismissed it airily. 'Everything happened in too much of a rush for you. It'll steady down in time. I think it's a case of good old-fashioned "can't make up your mindedness". *De mortuis* and all that apart, I don't think your little sister was quite the victim she liked to make out, and you're trying to reconcile what she told you with what you're finding out for yourself, and the two things don't always add up, do they? There's something else as well but I'm not going to pry into that. Why don't you go home and forget what you know of the past, it was all second hand stuff anyway. Concentrate on what you find out for yourself.

You've got it made, Kate,' Helen said bracingly. 'You hated the modelling bit and now you're out of it. No more swishing along the catwalk with everyone's eyes on you and no more photographic sessions in next to nothing. You are now a lady of leisure. Enjoy it! Be like me, if I paint something and I don't like it, I wipe it off, forget it and start again.'

'What do you do if the second try is as bad as the first?' asked Kate.

'Oh, love,' Helen's eyes grew troubled, 'husband trouble?'

Kate nodded mournfully, and suddenly Helen grew brisk. 'See,' she grabbed a piece of paper and a stick of charcoal. 'It's all a matter of emphasis.' Under her swift fingers the sketch grew until Jerome looked out of it, remote and arrogant. A couple of strokes and under Helen's fingers the arrogance grew while a bit of extra shading about the mouth produced an insufferable sneer. 'There, that's what emphasis does for you. Now, if I do this——' She started again and the face was quite pleasant this time; there was no sneer and the arrogance had been toned down.

Kate chuckled waterily. 'He looks like that when he's asleep,' she offered.

'Then only look at him while he's sleeping!' Helen made to screw up the sketch, but Kate stopped her.

'May I have it? I'd like to give it to his mother. I think that's the way she sees him.'

'There!' Helen crowed triumphantly. 'What did I tell you? It's all a matter of emphasis. If you dwell on the dark bits, you crowd out everything else.'

Coming back to the Kensington house, Kate felt much better, and even managed to greet Jerome with a smile.

'I've been to see Helen. She's very pleased you like

her sketch and quite thrilled that it's already hung. She's hoping for a few commissions from it. I had a look, but I think it's a bit idealised. She's made me look patient and long-suffering! Have you met the nurse yet? She's already installed. How's that for an obedient wife?' She thought she detected a flicker of humour in his eyes, but when she looked again they were shuttered and withdrawn.

Over dinner Kate heard herself being positively chatty, and when they went into the sitting-room she enquired brightly if he wanted to watch television. It turned out to be a horror film, full of vampires and ghouls with a great many corpses splashed with great gouts of blood, and she watched it avidly, trying to lose herself in the terror of it. When the last bloodstained victim had been avenged, Jerome switched off firmly.

'Don't make any plans beyond Friday.' He was tranquil. 'We're going up to Derbyshire to stay with my mother.'

'Oh no!' Unaccountably, Kate felt disappointed. 'We've only just got here and there's a lot to be done, the bedrooms and the little drawing-room. I was looking forward to that. Why do we have to go charging off almost as soon as we've arrived?'

'To collect Philip's puppy, of course.' He looked blandly at her and Kate's pleasant mood vanished as if it had been wiped out with a damp cloth.

'You're suspecting me,' she accused. 'I told you, I've been to Helen's. You can confirm it with Tobias, if you want. He took me there, parked outside the house where Helen lives and brought me straight back,' and with a snort of disgust, she rose and flounced out of the room.

Halfway up the stairs, Jerome caught her up, swinging an arm about her to halt her progress.

'You seemed very happy,' he observed, 'and you talked a lot over dinner. It's unusual.'

She glared at him. 'There's a law against being happy? I'll remember that! I'll also remember not to talk. I'll go about wearing a permanent scowl and speak in monosyllables in future.' Angrily she tried to wriggle free of his encompassing arm, but without success.

'Come to bed, Kate,' he ordered.

'I do not want to go to bed with you.' She enunciated every word with clarity through lips stiff with dislike and was surprised at herself. This wasn't the calm, quiet Kate Forrest who only twelve hours ago had thought that perhaps she was no longer hating her husband. She was hating now!

'I stipulated an obedient wife,' he reminded her.

'Then you shouldn't have married me,' she flared at him as she held the banister firmly with one hand, defying him to move her. 'I visited Helen and because I came home chatty, you're ready to suspect me of anything your foul mind can dredge up. And to crown it all, you're taking us up to the wilds of Derbyshire, which just proves that you don't trust me. I suppose you think I've been seeing Gerald—well, I haven't. Fetch Philip's dog, indeed!'

He slanted a dark glance down at her flushed, angry face and his eyes hardened. 'I'm also going to New York in seven to ten days' time, Kate, and I shall be away at least a week. I thought you'd be better with Mother than here on your own. You and she get on quite well, don't you?'

Kate refused to be mollified, a burning sense of injustice filled her, but despite her struggles she was drawn willy-nilly up the stairs and along the passage to the bedroom door. Jerome opened it and pushed her inside, where he clamped one arm about her, holding her firmly while his free hand tangled in her hair.

It was all too familiar by now. Kate knew what was

going to happen. He would kiss her until she went limp
in his arms. She would fight the animal warmth which
uncoiled inside her, she would fight it until it grew too
strong for her, until she wanted him to hold her, wanted
to be closer to him, wanted to be a part of him. A sob
rose in her throat as she felt herself softening and she
knew that in a very few moments she would be a
quivering mass of eagerness, that her arms would be
round him and that he could do what he liked with her.
She also knew that the laugh he would give would be
full of triumph. She cursed her own weakness until it
didn't matter any more, until his mouth and hands had
reduced her to pliancy. Then there was only the smooth
touch of his skin under her hands and against her body
and a wild exaltation that made her mouth greedy and
contented at one and the same time while his lips traced
a scorching path from her mouth to her breasts.

Kate woke to a grey dawn and decided mournfully
that she was no better than any of his other loves, except
of course that she was married to him. It was a consoling
thought until she tried to be honest with herself and
discovered that marriage in itself possibly wouldn't have
made very much difference. Jerome could make her
want him, married or not. That was a depressing
thought, and she frowned at it and wished she wasn't so
weak.

'Practising your scowl, Kate?' He asked the question
quietly without raising his head from the pillow, and
she turned to look at him.

'I've a bit of a headache,' she muttered. 'I think I'll
go and make some tea.'

His arm collected her and the grasp tightened about
her waist. 'Later,' he murmured. 'Go back to sleep now,
it's far too early.'

But she couldn't sleep. Something was knocking at

the doors of her mind, trying to get out. She knew very well what it was, but she wasn't going to let it out because it would hurt her—hurt her more than she had been hurt already, and it would go on hurting for ever and ever. In an effort to stop herself thinking about it, she examined his sleeping face. It wasn't really harsh, it was more like Helen's sketch, the nice one. He looked much younger asleep than this thirty-five years and his mouth was no longer a straight, hard line. It curved rather nicely and his eyelashes were long, thick and almost feminine. Even his hair was tumbled out of its normal brushed-back severity. Kate moved very gently so as not to wake him again because she didn't like his face so much when he was awake.

She finished writing her fifteenth letter of grateful thanks for a wedding present. This time it had been a Georgian silver salt cellar, it said so on the neatly typed list. Kate hadn't seen the article in question, but that didn't matter. She had written that it was beautiful and that she and Jerome would treasure it all their days. It was all true, she justified the letter. Georgian silver salt cellars were always beautiful and it ought probably to be locked up in a safe. The letter writing exhausted her, it was much more tiring than marking exercise books, and she laid down her pen and thought longingly of having a nice cup of tea and putting her feet up when Nanny mentioned in passing that Master Philip seemed to be growing out of all his clothes.

'But he can't be!' Kate was aghast. 'He had everything new just before the wedding, and that was only three weeks ago.'

'There, Mrs Jerome,' Nanny looked sickenly superior. 'Those were clothes for his holiday in Italy, they won't do for Derbyshire in March.'

Nanny Hogg was quite correct, the cuffs of Philip's

winter jumpers no longer covered his chubby wrists and
his dungaree-type trousers were definitely strained
around his portly middle.

Nanny surveyed him with pride. 'A nice solid little
boy,' she enthused. 'That's how I like my babies!'

Kate took comfort as she realised that she was no
longer bounded by a limited income and let Tobias
whisk them off to a large department store where one
thing led to another and she turned quite pale at the
amount of money she had spent. Things were arranged
to tempt the buyer, and after kitting Philip out and pur-
chasing sufficient wool to keep Nanny knitting for six
months or so, Kate fell for the temptation of pure silk
underwear, cashmere twin sets, soft wool dresses, silk
shirts, tailored suits and two soft, easy-fitting gowns for
evening wear at home. She came down to dinner in one
of them with a sheaf of bills in her hand and something
suspiciously like guilt on her face.

'I've spent a lot of money,' she told Jerome defiantly.
'I needn't have spent so much, I could have just bought
for Philip and collected some of my clothes from Helen,
she has them stored for me, but I didn't want to do
that.' She handed over the sheaf of bills ungraciously.
'There were other things—make-up, some perfume,
things like that, little things. I paid for those myself.'

Jerome flicked through the bills, his eyebrows raised
while she held her breath, thinking up things to say,
like, 'You'll be expected to have a well dressed wife' and
'I can always slop around in jeans if that's what you
want', but she had no opportunity of using these
phrases.

'Very economical.' He sorted the bills into two piles,
one for Philip's things which he pocketed, giving the
other pile back to her. There was the suspicion of a
smile about his mouth. 'Your allowance covers all that

easily and I don't expect you to clothe Philip out of it.'

For some unknown reason his generosity, instead of pleasing her or even making her feel relieved, made her cross and she spent the rest of the evening feeling like Oxfam. She was being donated to, and it took nearly all the pleasure out of spending so much money!

CHAPTER SEVEN

NANNY HOGG and Philip occupied the rear of the large car on the journey north and enlivened the trip with renderings of 'Ba Ba Black Sheep', 'The Grand Old Duke of York', 'Tom, Tom the Piper's Son' and other nursery ditties. When this palled, Nanny told stories from *Winnie the Pooh* and *Brer Rabbit* and various episodes from a heartrending tale of *The Little Boy who Didn't Look Where He Was Going*. Philip loved it, and as a proof, he refrained from being sick—although he recounted at length just how many times he had been sick before!

Kate therefore stepped from the car with no more than a faint crease in her skirt and decided that at times like these Nanny earned every penny of her considerable salary. Kate remembered previous journeys when she had stepped from the car, liberally bespattered with splashes from ice lollies and plastic cups of orange juice and feeling that she had been in intimate contact with a very grubby sweet-making factory.

Mrs Manfred's house was not far from Hathersage and quite close to the river, a lovely place, and Kate loved it on sight. She had been expecting and dreading a stately home, and breathed a soft sigh of relief when Jerome had stopped the car on the gravel drive outside this low, rambling, and obviously unstately dwelling. It didn't have the elegant perfection of the house in Kensington, it was solid, cosy and not at all fashionable. Jerome's mother wasn't fashionable either—not here. It was as if she had put off her skin of elegance here in this atmosphere and there was nothing to impede her direct tongue or her seemingly unfailing good humour.

She met them in the drive; clad in old fawn cord slacks which were tucked into the tops of muddy wellingtons, her upper half covered by an anorak so old and worn that the original green colour had become an indeterminate grey and her head covered with a bright spotted kerchief, tied gypsywise under her chin. She dropped the two plastic buckets which she was carrying and hurried towards them.

'There!' she smiled happily, 'and I was trying to get all my outside jobs done before you arrived. Hasn't the weather been foul? All this rain recently makes working outside a very chancy business, but I've nearly finished. Just the dogs left to feed.'

At the sound of the word 'dog', Philip's ears pricked and he adopted a pose which suggested that his short, fat little self was planted firmly in the gravel of the drive and he had no intention of being uprooted.

'Come for my dog,' he informed his grandmother, eyeing her suspiciously. 'Come in a car. Brm, brm!'

'And you shall have your dog, my lad.' Mrs Manfred looked at him and beneath her smile was a deep tenderness. Kate caught her breath at the look and forced herself to remember that Philip was Theo's son as well as Shirley's. The family resemblance was very strong and Mrs Manfred was probably tracing it and remembering when Theo was just this age. Jerome's mother left the two plastic buckets where they had dropped and held out a hand to her grandson. 'Come on then, Philip. We'll go into the house and see your dog. Jessie's been looking after him for you.'

'Jessie?' Philip wrinkled his brow at this extension of his little world, but he tucked his hand confidingly into his grandmother's.

'The thwarted mother,' Mrs Manfred shouted the

words to Kate over her shoulder. 'I told you about her, didn't I? The pup's been a godsend to us, we haven't had a bit of trouble with the old girl since he arrived.' As she was talking, she was leading them into the house, pausing in the porch to kick off her muddy wellingtons and disclosing in the process a pair of narrow, high-arched feet in darned khaki wool socks. 'I hope you're staying for a few weeks. Holly, that's another of my bitches, has just whelped, five lovely pups, and she's a very good mother. There'll be a nasty battle if Jessie goes interfering. On the other hand,' she paused thoughtfully, 'Tammy's about due to give birth in three weeks' time. Now, Tammy's *not* a good mother, anyone can look after her pups and the poor little things get so cold when she leaves them, so Jessie will be quite welcome in that pen. She'll save me pottering around with hot water bottles, so stay for a month, will you?'

'Mother is on her favourite hobbyhorse,' Jerome murmured to Kate, and he sounded amused. 'She has several, you know, and they all lead on to bigger and better things. This one leads to a consultation of the Kennel Club records, and then she'll discuss the good and bad points of every champion she's raised and how much more difficult it is to raise terrier champions than any other breed. Stop her now, before she really gets started, that's the only way.' He raised his voice slightly. 'Mother, this is Nanny Hogg. Nanny, my mother, Mrs Manfred. That ought to do it,' he dropped his voice and muttered in Kate's ear. 'Now they can talk babies!'

In the big, tidy kitchen of the house, by the side of a gleaming solid fuel cooker sat Philip's puppy in a lined basket, the side of which he was hopefully gnawing in search of nourishment. Philip gave a delighted yell of 'My dog!' and flopped down inside the basket with his puppy. A bright-eyed, hairy little face with tan ears,

sharply pricked, peered at the newcomer over the arm
of a chair and Kate experienced a moment's fear as a
middle-aged, rather rotund fox terrier heaved herself out
and went to investigate.

'Jessie,' Mrs Manfred was brief. 'No need to worry,
she won't hurt the boy, he's too young, and the silly old
fool can't tell the difference between pups and babies.'
Kate didn't believe it at first and kept a watchful eye on
the little group, but after a while she lost her fear and
turned away, leaving Philip and his dog together in the
basket under the watchful eye of the small terrier who
sat with pricked ears and a quivering tail, giving her
two charges alternate licks. Just in case anything went
wrong, Nanny Hogg sat herself firmly in the chair which
the dog had vacated and took over guard duty.

Mrs Manfred, who had by this time stripped herself
of her anorak, smiled an 'I told you so' smile and yelled,
'Hattie!' just as a gaunt, sour-looking woman came into
the kitchen.

'No need for you to yell your head off, Mrs Manfred,'
she scolded with the informality of long acquaintance.
'Tea'll be ready just as soon as you've fed those dogs
and got yourself tidy to sit down and eat it.' She rounded
on Jerome. 'So this is your new wife, eh? Well, you've
got better taste than I gave you credit for, my lad! Now,
you get off and feed those dogs. Leaving plastic buckets
all over the front of the house—I've never seen such a
thing! No better than gypsies!' Alternately scolding,
Hattie harried Jerome and his mother while she advanced
on Kate. 'Pleased to meet you, Mrs Jerome—and this is
young Philip again, is it? My, but he's grown, and down
with a dog, I see. Taking after his grandmother—well,
he can do worse than that. Dogs are friendly things and
good companions. I can't stand cats!'

'Hattie and I grew up together,' Mrs Manfred

confided as she led Kate upstairs to a big, old-fashioned bedroom. 'She looks as though she's made of lemon juice and vinegar, doesn't she? But it's only a look. Inside, she's as soft as marshmallow. Don't pay any attention to her scolding, she really doesn't mean a word of it.' She gestured round the room. 'Do you like it? I was born in this house, in this very bed. Of course, we didn't live here when Jerome's father was alive, we had a much bigger place near Buxton. That was what was wrong with it—too big, and not at all home like, so I brought Hattie and Theo back here. Jerome was quite grown up and always away at that time and there was more scope here for the dogs.'

Kate moved about the room, unpacking and hanging clothes away in the gigantic wardrobe while Jerome's mother talked on. Kate liked this house; it was a relief. She had been expecting something much more ornate, but here she felt relaxed and comfortable, at ease, and gradually her tension melted away so that she could give a genuine chuckle at some tale about the dogs or a humorous episode during a rehearsal of the local amateur dramatic society's production of *The Importance of Being Earnest*. When Jerome came upstairs later he found a Kate he'd never met before.

'Your mother's been telling me about the amateur dramatic society.' The face she turned to him no longer wore its mask of thinly veiled hostility. 'It sounds hilarious. I hope we're still here when the performance takes place. I'd love to see it.'

'It can be arranged.' Jerome's face was expressionless, although he was watching her closely.

'So much effort for just one performance!' Kate was still wrapped up in her own thoughts and hardly noticed his scrutiny. 'They all sound so keen and enthusiastic. Do you know that one man walks five miles to rehearsals, actually walks it, whatever the weather? That's a ten-mile round trip!'

'Wouldn't you walk five miles to do something you like doing?' Jerome sounded amused.

'Oh yes!' she assured him. 'But this isn't a young man, he's quite old, your mother says; well over sixty, yet he walks all that way! You'd think he'd stay home by the fire and watch T.V., especially if the weather was bad, but your mother says he never misses.'

'Mmm.' She surprised a lurking humour about his mouth. 'But you must remember that Mother's the stage manager. I don't think he dare miss.'

'Pooh!' she dismissed the thought. 'You're making your mother out to be some sort of a dragon, and she's nothing of the kind!'

'But I can remember when you thought of her as something much more unpleasant than a dragon,' he pointed out gently.

Kate's hands, which had been busy laying out underwear neatly in drawers, stilled as she took a breath.

'Yes, I did, didn't I?' She turned to face him squarely, her chin lifted and her green eyes steady on his. 'I shouldn't have allowed myself to form such an opinion on second-hand information. I was wrong, and I apologise for it.'

'That's generous of you, Kate.' She thought she detected a faint sneer about his mouth. It was so fleeting that she could not be quite sure, but it ruined her pleasant mood. Her back snapped straight and her eyes sparked.

'At least I'm apologising,' with an obvious effort she held her temper in check, 'and that's more than you've ever done to me. You thought that I was a promiscuous little trollop—and don't bother to deny it, because I know you did!' Her voice shook with indignation and her fingers clenched around the delicate garments she was holding. 'You even had the gall to admit that you hadn't expected me to be a virgin.' Her face flashed hotly at the memory. 'You've never apologised for thinking that about me, so don't look so high and mighty when I admit that I may have been wrong!' And gathering up her toilet bag and an assortment of flimsy underwear, she flounced out of the room and along the passage to the bathroom.

Kate inched her way through the door of the study with a tray of coffee neatly balanced on one hand, then, because her balancing act looked like falling apart, she grabbed the tray with her free hand and closed the door by putting her foot against it and pushing. She had determined to be useful and this was one of the few tasks which Hattie allowed her to do, the provision of elevenses.

'I can't sit around all day with my hands folded,' she had grumbled to the sour-looking housekeeper, 'and I don't get a look in with Philip nowadays, Nanny is too efficient. You'll have to find me something to do.'

Hattie had sniffed down her long, thin nose. 'I don't see as there's much you *can* do, Mrs Jerome, not to my way of thinking.' She wrinkled her forehead thoughtfully. 'There's the bit of dusting, if you wouldn't mind. That would give young Dodie more time for her vacuum cleaner, but I'm not having you in my kitchen. I can't bear people in my kitchen.'

Kate had been warned of Hattie's forthright tongue and after two days had accepted the dour-looking woman's scathing remarks. 'She was a sergeant cook with the Army during the war,' Mrs Manfred had explained. 'It gave her a feeling of power and she's never got over it. She treats us all as if we were privates and runs the place like a barracks. But she's a wonderful cook and a good friend as well, so we put up with her rough tongue for the sake of her warm heart.'

Jerome was deep in a pile of bills and receipts when she put the tray down on a side table, and he turned from the big, old-fashioned desk to look at her, gesturing ruefully.

'Mother gets her affairs into a muddle,' he encompassed the littered desk with a wave of his hand. 'I usually have to spend a couple of days sorting them out when I'm here.'

Kate nodded, although it was more a gracious inclination of the head than a nod, as she was still cross with him. 'It all looks very businesslike,' she commented remotely as she eyed the row of filing cabinets on the far wall.

His eyes followed hers. 'Not all Mother's,' he explained. 'A lot of it is mine, things I don't leave in the London office. Private things.' He accepted a cup of coffee and stirred it thoughtfully. 'The New York visit's been arranged and I'm going on Tuesday, would you like to come with me?'

Kate gave a delicate shudder. 'No, thank you. I seem to have been careering around like a person with no fixed abode ever since we were married. We were in Italy for ten days, London for four, and we've been here less than a week. I'm only just beginning to know where my things are instead of having to hunt through every drawer for a fresh pair of tights. Besides, there's Philip, he's only just settling down as well. You said we'd be here for a month, it wouldn't be fair to uproot him again for a couple of days.'

'Nanny will look after him while we're away, it's what she's paid for.'

Kate folded her lips firmly and glared. 'Nanny seems

to have him most of the time now, I hardly get a look in.' Trying to avoid further argument on what was to her a very sore subject, she nodded in the direction of the filing cabinets. 'You said these were your private things. Am I in there?'

'Not in those, Kate. In here.' Jerome pulled out a deep drawer in the desk to display a small suspended system containing labelled files. His long fingers riffled through the labels idly and stopped at one. 'Here it is—"KATE".' He extracted the slim folder, empty except for a brown manilla envelope sealed with a blob of red wax.

'Huh!' she snorted. 'That's not much. Is that all your nasty little men could dig up?'

'Only the most important things.' Negligently he slipped the file back into place and slid the drawer closed, locking it and putting his key ring back in his pocket. He slanted an odd smile at her. 'You could say they're my guarantees.'

'Guarantees?'

'That I have and will continue to have a loving, faithful and obedient wife.'

Kate picked up the coffee tray and resisting the desire to throw it at him, went to the door. 'Your best girlfriend's coming to dinner tonight, why don't you take *her* to New York?'

'Kate!' he exclaimed in a scandalised tone which was a mockery. 'How can you suggest such a thing? I'm a married man!'

'Oh, don't let that worry you,' she gave him a sickly sweet smile. 'I'm sure it wouldn't worry Estelle!' And she whisked herself out through the door and back to the kitchen, where she stood breathless for a few seconds before she went off to the sitting room to collect Mrs Manfred's empty cup.

At six o'clock, grubby and sticky from playing with

Philip and then helping him with his supper, Kate went off to get ready for dinner. She took her time over her bath and then wandered back into the bedroom, huddled in an old towelling bathrobe over her underwear, to decide what she was going to wear. Her fingers skipped along the hangers and stopped at one of the dresses which she had bought on the shopping spree in London. No, not this evening, she decided. This evening she wanted to be her own woman and wear clothes of her own providing. Estelle was going to be here and Kate wanted to feel free and not under an obligation to anybody.

Her fingers slid farther along and sorted out a green caftan. It was a favourite dress, although far from new. For all its simplicity, it had been ruinously expensive, but it was, she thought, one of those dresses that went anywhere and would come out of a case looking as though it had been freshly pressed—a dark green drifting silk, loose and comfortable, and the whole relieved only by a narrow edging of tiny gilt bead embroidery around the neck and the wide sleeves. Carefully she detached the hanger from the rod and then stood looking at the dress, deep in thought.

She had worn this dress for work once, been photographed in it for an advertisement for a dishwasher, the sort of thing where an elegant, beautifully groomed woman was pictured in a gigantic and immaculate kitchen, with one redly lacquered fingernail pressing the START button and leading everybody to suppose that the mere possession of such a piece of equipment would ensure that household drudgery was a thing of the past and that any kitchen graced with its presence would immediately assume the proportions of the mock-up around her. The advertisement had appeared in several glossy magazines, she remembered—and if she remembered, so might others.

Sadly she restored the green caftan to its hanger and brought out in its stead a long, black skirt in heavy, thick silk. It would cling to her hips and flare around her ankles, and somewhere there was a blouse to go with it; her fingers flicked again until she came to it. Very straightlaced, she thought, examining the high neck decorated with a frill of lace and the long full sleeves, gathered into tight cuffs. There was nothing of Noelle Lowe about this outfit and she forced an enthusiastic smile as she sat down at the dressing table and started on her face and hair.

Jerome came wandering in just before seven. He was in shirt sleeves, but even so he looked very impressive. His thin black trousers made his long legs look even longer, and Kate sighed with disgust. Even wearing her highest heels, she still wouldn't be able to look him straight in the eye, she would still be looking up at him.

'Can you?' he gestured with the black tie he was holding in his fingers. 'Mother's very traditional, we have to be properly dressed for one of her dinner parties, no matter how small.'

'Mmm.' She rose and came to stand behind him. 'Oh, for heaven's sake, sit down,' she scolded. 'I can't reach up there.'

Obligingly, he subsided on to the dressing stool and while she was making a neat bow he looked at her in the mirror. 'Did you do this often?' His grey eyes held hers in the reflection and her fingers hesitated. 'Your father?' he suggested.

'No,' she smiled reminiscently. 'Daddy was a heathen. He didn't like dressing up, and when he had to, he wore one of those made-up things which clipped at the back. I had to learn to do this once for a television commercial. It took me nearly a week to learn the trick of it. You have to pretend you're tying a bow on your own neck. . . .' Her voice faded to a husky whisper as he reached up and caught her arms, pulling her round until she lost her balance and stumbled on to his knee, where he held her chin and kissed her thoroughly, forcing her response. When he raised his head, he examined her face closely.

'That's better.' He sounded satisfied. 'Now you look like a bride of a few weeks!'

'And I'll have to do my face and hair all over again!' she was almost crying. 'You've messed them up!'

'A sweet disorder,' he quoted, and then with raised eyebrows, 'Shakespeare?'

'Herrick,' Kate contradicted savagely as she pushed away from him and from the mirror and scrubbed at her slightly swollen lips with a tissue.

'And what's this?' Jerome's fingers flicked at the black skirt and white blouse where they lay ready on the bed. 'We're going to a small dinner party, not a fancy dress ball.'

'It's what I'm wearing,' she was defiant, 'and it's not fancy dress.'

He made a disgusted sound and swung around to the wardrobe, swinging the door wide and rattling the hangers on the rod. Finally he turned with the green caftan in his hands.

'Wear that!'

'No.' There was an obstinate line about her mouth. 'You don't understand. I've worn that dress for an advert. I was photographed in it. Somebody might remember. Your best girl-friend, for instance. She'd love that!'

'And?' He raised one black eyebrow.

'And then it'll be all over Derbyshire in no time flat. The great Jerome Manfred married a model. Neither you nor your mother will appreciate that.'

'We shan't be disturbed about it.' He smiled quite a nice smile and Kate caught her breath at the sight of it. 'Don't be a fool, Kate. There are some things you can't hide, and dressing up to look like a superior Edwardian nursery governess isn't going to hide them either. Gossip doesn't worry me, and I can assure you it doesn't bother my mother. Wear the green thing. It'll suit you.'

Although she had wanted to wear the green dress, the very fact that she had been practically ordered to do so filled her with rage. Jerome dictated where they should go, how and where they should live, how she should spend her spare time, and now he was telling her how to dress, what to wear, so that she slid the caftan over her head with a very bad grace, and though she knew it suited her and she both looked and felt good in it, she was still raging when she went down the stairs with him.

Four pairs of eyes turned in her direction as she entered the drawing room, and she was vaguely comforted by the pressure of Jerome's hand at her waist. His mother smiled at her benignly; his mother's old friend, the military man who had given her away, now gave her an appreciative twinkle; the young up-and-coming barrister chosen as a partner for Estelle gave her an assessing glance, and Estelle herself didn't bother to conceal her dislike or disinterest. Kate turned to her husband with a sugary smile.

'Introduce me, darling,' she said huskily. 'I know everybody was at the wedding, but I'm hopeless at names, you know that. There are times when I hardly remember my own.' Her lips were smiling, but her eyes were full of a passionate rage and glowed very green between her dark lashes while she fulminated inwardly. Throughout the rest of the evening, she continued to fulminate, although nothing of it showed on her face.

Three years of teaching had taught her a variety of

expressions, and she used them all—polite pleasure, polite enquiry, polite attention and polite disbelief. She accepted her small glass of sweet sherry with polite pleasure, although she disliked alcohol in most forms; she treated the military gentleman's reminiscences of desert warfare with polite attention and some of his more outrageous tales brought on polite enquiry; while Estelle's continued remarks on the closeness of the bond between herself and Jerome, how they had grown up together and had shared everything, made Kate assume the appearance of polite disbelief. Estelle, she judged, couldn't be more than twenty at the most, so Jerome had been verging on the young man stage when the girl was kicking and blowing bubbles in her pram. She looked at Estelle with something akin to pity. It was hard for her to see such a lovely young thing making such a fool of herself and not be able to do a thing about it. Kate shook her head and returned her attention to her dinner, which was very good indeed.

She worked her way through iced grapefruit, a delicate cheese soufflé duck à l'orange, and a pineapple sorbet in Kirsch with the dedication of a true gourmet and enjoyed every mouthful because she had a normal, healthy appetite. She didn't see why she should allow Estelle's little poisonous darts and barbs to ruin good food.

After dinner, Mrs Manfred decided to play whist, and her military friend backed her up. There was nothing like a pleasant game of cards after a good dinner and his eyes had twinkled bright blue at Kate, but Kate had to decline. If they wanted another couple, they would have to look farther than herself. She could not play cards, not properly, she could offer Ludo and Snakes and Ladders, but that was all. At cards she was stupid, she explained, and had on several occasions when she had been forced into playing been responsible for unseemly quarrels and disgraceful shows of temper on the part of her partners. So Mrs Manfred commandeered her son and the up-and-coming young barrister because Estelle had suddenly developed an unaccountable headache and was no longer able to concentrate.

The four players adjourned to a table in the window embrasure and settled down to a cut-throat game in an earnest silence broken only by Jerome's mother, who held post-mortems on every hand and pointed out everybody's mistakes with a complete disregard for their feelings which put Kate strongly in mind of her husband in one of his most arrogant moods. Kate sat in a corner of the couch, her toes toasting because she was too near the fire, and after a while Estelle joined her.

'Isn't he tired of you yet?' Kate gave an inward gasp at the sheer effrontery of the question while she schooled her lips to a sweet smile.

'No, not yet,' she murmured softly, although she knew that the four at the card table could not hear. 'I'm afraid you'll have to wait a little longer.'

'Oh, it won't be long now.' Estelle preened herself, her hands patting her hair into a smooth black cap about her ears. 'I said you wouldn't last long, and I'm always right about Jerome's fancy women. But you must be noticing the difference already, surely.'

Kate shook her head, dumb with shock. She closed her eyes and tried hard to pretend that this wasn't happening.

'There's one consolation for you,' Estelle continued with venom. 'Jerome's quite generous. He'll make it worth your while.'

Kate sat quite still, hardly believing her ears. Nobody, but nobody could possibly talk like this, think like this! The girl must be mad. She stole a sideways look at

Estelle and shook her head slightly. No, the girl wasn't mad, not in the accepted sense. Perhaps she'd been watching too much bad television or reading ridiculous novels; she sounded like the worst kind of soap opera. Since there seemed to be no way of stopping her, Kate decided to enter into the spirit of the thing. After all, she consoled herself, she ought to be able to win this stupid exchange, she had read many more books than Estelle!

'I'm very expensive,' she answered, keeping her sweet smile going. 'I don't think I could afford to settle for less than a million.'

'You won't get that much.' Estelle took the discussion very seriously. 'A few thousand perhaps, I could possibly talk Jerome into that.'

Kate sighed. 'Why are millionaires so mean? I give him the best years of my life and he expects to buy me off with a few thousands. It's chicken feed! No, Estelle, I'm afraid it'll have to be a million. I have to look at things in a very practical way. I've grown to like luxurious living and I don't fancy going back to the rat-race of being a photographic model. I'm not getting any younger and the competition is fierce, believe me. There are always at least half a dozen lovely young things eager and willing to do almost anything to take my place.'

'Mmm,' Estelle nodded sagely. 'But that cuts both ways, doesn't it? I mean, in two or three years' time you'll begin to look your age. It's different for me, two years will only make me twenty-one, there won't be any lines on my face, in fact I shan't have aged at all. Perhaps it would be better for you to go now; later on, Jerome mightn't give you so much.'

Kate sat quietly, her expression relaxed and friendly. To the casual observer, she was merely a good-looking young woman enjoying a casual conversation, but anybody looking more closely would have seen her fingers clenched so that the nails were cutting into the skin. She was keeping a hard hold on herself, and one more of Estelle's silly remarks was going to either make her explode with ungovernable rage or burst into hysterical laughter, either of which would cause a humiliating scene. Fortunately, she was spared another exchange when Mrs Manfred turned from the table.

'What are you two talking about?' Her attention was no longer on the cards and when her military friend held the pack out for her to cut, she waved them aside. 'We'll finish now anyway, Jerome isn't keeping his mind on the game and I can't stand playing with a partner who isn't giving his full attention to the cards.' She turned again towards the couch and repeated her question. 'What have you two been talking about?'

Kate recalled a Western film which she had seen and smiled at her mother-in-law. 'We're playing a peculiar game of poker, without cards. Estelle's staking a couple of thousand, but I'm raising the ante.'

'How high?' Jerome looked across at her, a slight frown between his brows.

'One million,' she returned composedly.

'And what's in the kitty?' The frown had gone and now he looked lazily amused.

'You are, darling!' she answered him demurely.

When the last nightcaps had been drunk and the visitors had left, Kate bade her mother-in-law a warm goodnight and began to climb the stairs. Half way up, she was overcome by the nonsensical conversation with Estelle and dissolved into giggles. She was still giggling when she slipped into bed.

'What's so amusing?' Jerome had come back from the bathroom, his shower robe his only garment, and sat himself on the side of the bed.

Kate wagged her head; she couldn't trust herself to speak, it would all have been nonsense anyway.

'Was it something Estelle said?'

Suddenly Kate found that there was nothing funny about it any more and her paroxysm of giggles stopped as if they were part of another person. She sat quite still, looking at him, waiting.

'Was that what the peculiar conversation was about, the thousands and your million? Did Estelle offer you money?'

Kate lifted her chin disdainfully. 'No, she didn't offer me money, not her own. She offered me yours, a couple of thousand of it, so I told her it wasn't enough.'

'What was it for, an escape?' His hand closed over her arm, the fingers tightening until she flinched.

'An escape!' She giggled again, this time rather hysterically. 'No, I've been about as humiliated as it's possible to be. Your girl-friend offered to get me a couple of thousand as a pay-off when you're tired of me. She said I could count on your generosity, but not above a couple of thousand.' Her mouth twisted bitterly. 'It's nice to know one's cash value, isn't it? Has she done this sort of thing for you before, I wonder? She certainly handled it with a good deal of aplomb. Well, you can tell her from me that when you let me go, that'll be payment enough for me. I shan't ask for a penny. I've kept myself before and I can do it again. I don't need hand outs from the Manfreds!' By this time Kate had worked herself into a fine temper and the last words came out almost as a snarl.

The grip on her arm did not lessen as Jerome calmly leaned across and took her other arm and shook her with just sufficient force to make her gasp. 'Be quiet, Kate! Estelle was on her own business, not mine, as you very well know, if you'll be quiet and think reasonably about it. I told you before we married that I didn't envisage divorce, and you remember that, I know. There's no escape for you, my dear, either with or without a pay-off. I'm very well content with my wife.' And without further ado, he tossed off his robe and joined her in bed. Kate turned her back on him and scolded into her pillow:

'Then tell your girl-friend to keep her claws covered when she meets me in future!'

With one hand he turned her to face him while with the other he reached out and switched off the light. In the darkness, she felt his warm breath on her face as he chuckled, 'Jealous, Kate?'

CHAPTER EIGHT

IT was a grey day with lowering clouds and a gusting wind to drive them when Jerome made his departure for New York. It wasn't raining, although it looked as if it wanted to, and, according to Hattie and her barometer which she believed in preference to the weather-forecast, it would rain as soon as the wind dropped.

Kate, holding a struggling Philip, watched the car vanish down the drive and then turned with a shiver to re-enter the house where Nanny would be waiting to take Philip away and feed him cough medicine. Kate was rather glad of this. Philip had wanted to go with his uncle and his childish mind could see no reason why this should not be so, therefore he was disappointed and in consequence, cross and badly behaved. She had been holding him up in her arms so that he should see the car for as long as possible and he had been kicking his slippered feet in disgusted misery at being left behind and Kate's solar plexus had suffered. Yes, Nanny was the best person to deal with Philip in this mood!

Hattie met them just inside the door, thrusting a coffee tray into her hands and scolding Mrs Manfred, who was following.

'You'll catch your deaths, prancing around outside in this weather, waving goodbye to a lad who'll only be gone four days! I've never heard of such sentimental nonsense. Drink your coffee, Mrs Manfred, and then away with you down to the kennels. That Jessie's been up to her tricks again, she came in as bold as brass with a pup she's stolen while you had your back turned. I've got it in the kitchen now, wrapped up in a piece of flannel until you can take it back.'

Hattie harried and nagged unmercifully until her mistress had drunk the coffee and was striding back to the kennels with the purloined puppy, her wellingtons making squelchy noises on the gravel path. When she had gone, Hattie turned her attention to Kate. 'And what's the matter with you this morning, may I ask? I've just been upstairs and that's no way to leave a bedroom, clothes all over the place! A place for everything and everything in its place, that's my motto and you'd do well to observe it. Under the bed's no place for a nightgown, Mrs Jerome!' and with a disapproving snort, she seized the tray and marched back to the kitchen.

Kate towed an obstreperous Philip back upstairs to the nursery. He was like a record with the needle stuck in one groove, 'Uncle gone in a car, brrm, brrm,' until they reached the landing, when he suddenly spread his arms and zoomed off down the passage doing his impression of a jet engine, 'Fly in a jumbo, wheeeeeeh!' Thankfully, Kate handed him over to Nanny, who after duly admiring his imitation of a small, fat aeroplane, gave him his cough syrup and settled him down with several plastic toys.

'Such a pity Mr Manfred has to be away, if only for a few days,' the small, rotund woman heaved a sentimental sigh. 'We grow to depend on our menfolk, don't we?'

Kate frowned. Nanny had adopted the 'We' habit. She turned up at odd moments with Philip, saying 'We have torn our little shirt beyond repair' or 'We have a nasty little cough this morning'. Now she was saying 'We are missing our menfolk', or words to that effect, and it wasn't true! Kate wasn't missing her menfolk. He had only been gone for an hour and she was looking forward to these four days of freedom. Days when she would be able to do, say and wear exactly what she liked. She certainly wouldn't be missing him! Only it didn't work out that way.

Late in the afternoon, as Hattie had predicted, the wind dropped and it started to rain, a steady downpour which made walks with Philip impossible, and Hattie frowned on Kate's choice of clothes, a faded pair of jeans and a very sloppy jumper.

'That's no dress for a lady's drawing room,' she remarked tartly when in the afternoon she found Kate sprawled on the couch, munching an apple and trying to whip up a little enthusiasm for an extremely boring book. 'Look at you!' she made it sound disgusting. 'Your hair all anyhow and tied back with a piece of frayed ribbon and those jeans fit only for the rag bag! Upstairs with you and make yourself decent before I set the tea. I don't know what Mr Jerome would say if he could see you now!'

'But he can't,' Kate was triumphant. 'He's away for four days!'

'More's the pity,' the housekeeper spoke with finality. 'The sooner he's back, the better! A sloppy mistress makes a sloppy maid, and the next thing will be young Dodie wanting to wear jeans to push her vacuum cleaner.'

After dinner, Kate had been looking forward to a pleasant chat with her mother-in-law about amateur dramatics, the surrounding countryside and/or dogs, but this was not permitted. Kate cursed her own folly in first finding the sketch which Helen had made of Jerome and then giving it to his mother, for after dinner Mrs Manfred excused herself for a few moments and then reappeared staggering under the weight of several large photograph albums. Jerome's mother was going to enjoy a nostalgic evening browsing among acres of memories and, willy-nilly, Kate was to accompany her on this trip to the past. Much later, as she clambered into the wide, lonely-looking bed, it was with the firm conviction that Jerome looked just as arrogant and self-sufficient in his christening robe as he did nowadays!

There was one small brush with Estelle which took place on the second day of Jerome's absence. Kate was wrapped up firmly in a waterproof and was cheerfully plodding along the narrow lanes to Hathersage where Nanny had ordered her to purchase some buttons for the cardigan being knitted for Philip. It wasn't a long walk and Kate was enjoying it when a red sports car pulled up alongside her. Estelle leaned across from the driver's seat and opened the door.

'Get in,' she commanded savagely, and when Kate obliged, she sat staring through the windscreen, making no attempt to drive on.

'I have to buy some things in Hathersage for Nanny.' Kate was gentle. 'I'd like to get there before the shops close.'

Estelle ignored it. 'Why haven't you gone?' she demanded. 'There's nothing to stop you now.'

The inside of the low-slung car was claustrophobic and Kate felt as though she was surrounded by a thick black cloud of violence.

'I know about you.' Estelle set the car in motion. 'Jerome isn't the only one who can make enquiries. I know he only married you to get Philip.' At Kate's look of surprise, the girl grinned with savage satisfaction. 'I'm quite well acquainted with a past friend of yours, not so friendly now, I'm sorry to say; I made it my business to get acquainted, so I know all about you. Get out now, while you can.'

'I can't do that.' Kate leaned back wearily in the seat.

She found even a few minutes with Estelle very exhausting, there was so much violence about the girl, ill-controlled violence.

'Why not? You're nothing special,' Estelle's hands tightened on the steering wheel and her foot jabbed down hard on the accelerator. 'Don't you realise there've been dozens of women like you? Jerome likes a bit of amusement, and that's all you are to him, a bit of amusement. You don't mean a thing!'

The car bucketed round a corner much too fast and Kate felt the rear end skid slightly. This was definitely not the time to aggravate Estelle further. The girl was like a wild thing, snapping and clawing, uncaring of whom she hurt. Kate shut her mouth firmly, closed her eyes for the rest of the short journey and got out of the car in Hathersage conscious only of relief that she had emerged from the ride, unhurt and in one piece. But Estelle couldn't leave the matter rest.

'Why don't you go?' she hissed the question through the open door of the car. 'I've told you, you're only one in a long string. I'll help you if you can't manage by yourself.'

Kate shook her head. 'I can't,' she said gently. 'He married me!' And then she stepped back swiftly as Estelle slammed the door and started off in one jerky movement which threatened to leave Kate a bleeding and broken mess in the gutter. She stood watching the tail lights receding and felt a mild surprise at herself. Not once during the altercation had she even thought about Philip! Here had been the opportunity to get away and perhaps, if she was lucky, take the boy with her, and she had refused it. She must be mad, quite mad!

Jerome came home on Saturday and on the following Monday she and he paid a flying visit to the Kensington house. Jerome had put his foot down firmly and with force. Philip was not coming. He was quite reasonable and logical about it.

'Philip stays here. He has his nanny, his grandmother, Hattie and Dodie. How many more women are needed to care for one small boy for a few days?'

'I want him with me.' Kate had also been firm, only Jerome didn't call her firmness 'firm', he had given it another name.

'Don't be obstinate, Kate. We're going down to see what the decorators have done and to choose the rest of the furniture. Philip will only be in the way. . . .'

'Philip is never in the way,' she raged quietly.

'. . . . and the upset and the travelling won't be good for him,' Jerome continued as though she hadn't spoken. 'He stays here!' He raised his eyebrows as she turned a furious face on him. 'Be reasonable and if you won't consider Philip, consider Nurse Hogg. She's not a young woman. . . .

'She needn't come,' Kate interrupted. 'I can look after him myself.'

'. . . . and the travelling, the constant attention our nephew demands? The poor woman will be exhausted.' Once again it was as though she hadn't interrupted him. 'And don't say that if Philip doesn't go, you won't go, because you *will* go, if I have to carry you out to the car and tie you in the seat.'

Kate was not stupid, she knew when she was beaten, and she was also honest enough to admit to herself, but only to herself, that Jerome was correct. She remembered vividly Philip, tired and cross on the plane from Rome to London, she recalled the appalling mess in the back of the car on the journey up from Bodmin, and she mused over Nanny's inexhaustible patience and unfailing good humour in keeping the little boy happy and amused on the way from London to Derbyshire. So she gave way as gracefully as possible, although she made it sound definitely grudging.

'All right, if that's the way you want it.'

'That is just the way I want it,' he sounded even more arrogant than ever, 'and therefore that's the way it will be. An obedient wife,' he slanted a dark grey look down at her, 'doesn't fight her husband every inch of the way, and that's what you've been doing, Kate, even before we were married. I've given way when I thought you had reason on your side, but this time your demand is unreasonable.' He paused and then resumed in a very definite tone, 'We shall do our business more quickly and more comfortably without Philip, so he will *not* be coming.'

At the Kensington house, the two bedrooms and the small drawing-room looked wonderful. Kate said so and Mrs Davies sniffed disparagingly.

'So they should, madam. I've had our Ellen scrubbing away at them every day since those men left. Call themselves a firm of decorators? You should have seen the mess they made, not to mention two strips of paper in the drawing-room put on upside down. But everything's ready now and I've had samples of the colours left so you can match up for carpets and drapes.'

'The spare bedrooms are a bit small,' Kate smiled across the dinner table at her husband. Mrs Davies's cooking might be old-fashioned, but it was superb, and Kate, who had been hungry, now felt replete, warm and content so that everything around her was likeable, even Jerome. 'Do you think fitted units would be better than ordinary wardrobes, dressing tables and such?'

He paused in lighting a cigarette and regarded her through a faint cloud of blue smoke. 'You'll please yourself, Kate. It's your home.'

She agreed happily. 'They're guest rooms, so I think fitted units would look better; they'd leave more space. How funny,' she marvelled, 'me bothering about space as if I was used to acres and acres of it—but that's what luxury living does for you. I remember when Shirley first came to my little flat. . . .'

'We will not discuss your stepsister.' From a moderately pleasant human being, Jerome turned immediately into a dark, withdrawn tyrant, and she bristled.

'Why not? What have you got against Shirley? When I think of the way your family treated her—you had her investigated as if she was no better than a shoplifter, Theo left her. . . .'

With an angry growl, he slammed down his napkin and sat back in the chair. 'Theo did *not* leave her!'

'He did!' Kate scowled. 'Shirley came to me. . . . He left her because she was pregnant and wasn't looking pretty any more. She told me!'

'Your little sister told you a great many things, Kate, and very few of them were the truth.' He looked at her bleakly and his face was hard. 'For instance, did she tell you that she didn't want the child?'

'That's not true!' Kate exploded, the last of her pleasant feelings towards him vanishing like silk going up in flames.

'It was true,' he ignored her violent protest. 'I told you once before that you were deaf as well as blind. Shirley had made an appointment at a private clinic to have an abortion, Theo found out about it and whipped her up to Mother's for a month. The young fool thought she'd done it because she was young and frightened! He thought Mother could talk some sense into her. When he found she'd calmed down and apparently accepted the baby coming, he gave way and brought her back to London. Only it didn't stop there.' He raised a hand to

silence Kate's outburst. 'Your little sister went back to
the clinic as soon as Theo's back was turned, but fortunately for Philip, she was too late. The doctors
wouldn't touch her and, I imagine for pure spite, she
landed herself on you. She knew Theo wanted the baby
and that's how she punished him for making her have
it. She disappeared without a word.'

Kate sat, white-faced, and let the words run over her.
They were horrible things Jerome was saying, horrible!
But somehow she knew they were true. Whatever other
bad points he had, he didn't lie. He might be arrogant,
insensitive and withdrawn; he might have—he *had*
forced her into marriage, used blackmail to do it, he
had held those negatives over her head like a sword of
Damocles, he had bullied and threatened to get his own
way, but he didn't stoop to barefaced lies.

'You could have traced her,' she whispered through
the pain in her throat and he smiled at her, it wasn't a
nice smile.

'Yes, I could have traced her. I'm not so nice in my
dealings as Theo was. He was little more than a boy,
remember, only a few months older than your sister and
full of silly chivalrous notions. Yes, as you say, I could
have traced her, but I was over in the States. It was a
busy time and Mother wouldn't allow Theo to bother
me, we were just getting the New York Office off the
ground. He tried to do it on his own, but he wore kid
gloves to do it and he couldn't be detached enough.
Shirley used to send him a photograph every month
after Philip was born, one of those quickie things taken
in a booth. There was no way of tracing those, either.'
Jerome rose to his feet and came around the table, seiz-
ing her and dragging her to her feet, his fingers closing
cruelly on her shoulders. 'He was a nice kid, Kate, barely
twenty! How would you have felt if somebody had sent

you a photograph of *your* son once a month, tormented you with *that*? Did you ever meet Theo?'

Kate opened her mouth to say that of course she'd met Theo, but the words never came, as she realised with a sick feeling in her stomach that she never had. It seemed almost impossible, but it was true. Theo had been so clear in her mind, and yet the image had all been built from a few photographs and the things Shirley had said. 'No,' she said dully, 'I never met him.'

There was a wry look about Jerome's mouth. 'He was a bit wild and careless, but he settled down when he married. Mother said that marriage seemed to have made a man of him. Do you want to accuse my mother of lying, Kate?'

She shook her head. 'No,' she whispered. 'Your mother doesn't lie. But it can't have been as bad as you say. Shirley went back to him.'

She peeped upwards and the face that looked back down at her was that of a stranger, hard and masklike, with white patches about the nose and mouth and a dreadful bitter look in the eyes.

'Mmm, but on her terms.' It was almost a sneer. 'There were to be no more children—your little sister was too sensitive, too delicate to endure such a disgusting procedure again. Theo had to make sure that there would be no further recurrence, she insisted on it. After all, as she pointed out, he now had a son, he didn't want more!'

'Oh, no!' Tears were streaming down Kate's face. 'Not that!'

'Precisely that! And he did it for her,' Jerome's fingers were digging into her shoulders, almost crushing the slender bones, but she hardly felt the pain, all she could think of was the horror she felt. Jerome shook her and she paid no attention. 'Can you wonder he idolised the boy,' his voice was cold and cutting. 'His boy, his son, the only one he'd ever have! And when he finally put his foot down and got rid of the permanent nanny Shirley had installed, when he was going to take his wife and son on holiday, she wouldn't even let him have that. She brought the boy to you.'

'Shirley said it was a second honeymoon. . . .' Kate had stopped crying and stood, cold and empty, her face paper-white. 'Couldn't you have stopped it, Theo's op, I mean?'

'Your little sister's timing was too good,' he was jeering at her. 'She had it arranged very nicely. It was all over and they were back living together when I returned from the States.'

Kate lay huddled into herself on her own side of the bed that night. Not even the electric blanket could disperse the cold which had invaded every inch of her body. She searched around in her mind for some extenuating circumstances, something, anything which would explain Shirley's behaviour, some little excuse, any excuse for her sister's complete disregard for anything but her own interests. Shirley had been very young, of course, and she had been a beautiful child, so that everybody had spoiled her a little. Kate's mind went on hunting, ferreting, and she was still awake much later when Jerome came to bed. She lay in a huddle of misery, feeling the movement as he slid between the sheets. He hated her, he *must* be hating her. He wouldn't even want to touch her!

Her misery increased because she had at last to admit to herself the unadmittable thing and she couldn't bear it. Not to lie here beside this man, her husband; to want the comfort of his arms about her, wanting to creep closer to him, to hold him and to give him whatever comfort and solace he could find in her willing body.

This was a fine time to discover that she loved her husband!

'Stop crying, Kate.'

'I'm not crying.' It was the truth. She was long past tears and it was too late for tears. Was this, then, why Jerome had married her? Not only to get Philip but to make her pay for the pain Shirley had inflicted on the Manfreds as she went on her heedless, uncaring way!

Kate thought of leaving and a bitter little smile twisted her mouth. She couldn't leave, she knew that. Not unless he threw her out. He'd taught her all she knew about loving a man and a life without him would be a dreary waste, a cold arid desert where she would wander, for ever alone, knowing what heaven was like and never being able to find it again.

On impulse she turned over to face him, her hand going out to touch his body, and the skin felt like silk against her fingers. 'I'm sorry,' but even as she spoke, she knew it was useless. There was no comfort she could give him and he was in no mood to comfort her.

'Go to sleep, Kate.' He sounded unutterably weary, and with a little whimper of pain, she turned again, away from him, and lay quietly in the darkness, feeling very much alone and outcast.

In the morning, her pain had subsided to a dull ache and although she still felt bad, the daylight helped. During her shower and while she was dressing, she looked at what was to be her life and shuddered. It would be a chill, hopeless hell. It would be interspersed, of course, with bursts of hot passion, but passion without love wouldn't be a very satisfactory thing; there would be no tenderness, no companionship. While she had thought that she hated Jerome, that sort of life was survivable, but not now. Now she wanted more, and she would never get it. She would just have to make do with what she had, because it was better than living without him. She nodded at her reflection and went sedately down to breakfast.

Jerome was already there, calmly eating bacon and kidneys, and the face he raised to her was dark and withdrawn. He was wearing his mask. Last night she had seen sorrow and hurt in his eyes, but this morning those same eyes were quiet and unfathomable.

'How soon can you be ready?' It was an impersonal question.

'I'm ready now.' She took a sip of scalding coffee and felt better for it, raising cool green eyes to his. 'While we're in London, I'd like to see Helen, if there's time.'

'Mmm.' He returned his attention to the paper and spoke through it. 'We can extend our stay for another day, if necessary.'

The shopping helped as well. Even the mundane purchase of carpets, curtaining and bedroom units helped to take Kate's mind away from her private grief. She drew his attention to a carpet sample in a dark moss green with a looped pile. He fingered it briefly and frowned.

'The other sample is of a better quality.'

'I know,' she wrinkled her forehead, 'but this is just the right shade. Why can't we have it, even though it doesn't cost as much and it probably won't wear as well? It's for a guest bedroom and it won't have a lot of wear, and with what we save on this, we can buy that beautiful Chinese washed thing I thought would be too expensive. That would look lovely in the little drawing-room.'

'Are you becoming thrifty, Kate?' She breathed a soft sigh of relief. Jerome was sounding nearly human again. Tolerable!

'I've always been thrifty,' she scolded gently. 'I was born with a cheeseparing disposition.' She stopped abruptly because she had been going to say that Shirley had always said so. He said it for her.

'That's what Shirley always said?' And she nodded dumbly.

They lunched in a small French restaurant near Marble Arch and afterwards continued the buying spree until four o'clock, when he put her in a taxi, giving the driver Helen's address.

'Won't you come?' She was hesitant.

'No, not this time. I've one or two things to attend to. I'll call for you at six. Will you have finished your girlish gossip by then?'

'Oh, I think so,' and she gave him what she hoped was a radiant smile as he closed the door of the cab and stepped back on to the pavement.

Helen was at home and in high spirits. She dragged Kate into the big shabby studio room and pushed her into the velvet-covered chair which was used for sittings.

'You're my good luck piece.' Helen sounded on top of the world. 'Hang on there while I make some coffee. Don't go away whatever you do. I've sold two pictures,' she chortled as she came back in, balancing the coffee mugs on a old palette, 'and I had a phone call from your ma-in-law. She wants a miniature of Philip and she's invited me up there later in the year to do it. What do you think of that?'

Kate put her sorrow aside for the moment to enter into Helen's joy. 'That's marvellous! Which ones did you sell?'

'That one of the Moor, the winter scene, do you remember it? And the one of the ponies, and I've been offered a really impressive place for my next showing, not up a furtive little back street like the last one. I tell you, Kate, I've broken through at last.' She beamed and heaved a contented sigh. 'Five years,' she marvelled, 'and at last I've made it. Just think of the difference it will make. Good brushes; new, really new canvases and with a bit more luck, no more waitressing at the café on the corner.'

'Toulouse-Lautrec. . . .' Kate began, but her words were brushed aside.

'Yes, I know, but he wasn't waitressing. He didn't have to stagger round with plates of steak and kidney pud, and I bet nobody ever pinched his bottom when he was trying to clean a table.' Helen shook her head violently. 'He was a customer.' Then she giggled. 'Think what a mess he'd have been in today! No nice white tablecloths to draw on. I'd like to have seen him staggering home with a melamine top! How are you anyway? You'll have to forgive me, but I get so carried away with success that I forget my manners. You look a bit drawn, love. Anything wrong?'

Kate looked down at her coffee mug as though it was a gypsy's crystal ball; she hesitated, but only fractionally. 'Yes, there's something very wrong,' she muttered. When she raised her eyes to Helen, there were no tears in them, but they looked drowned. 'You remember telling me once that you thought Shirley wasn't quite the victim I believed——' She hesitated again. 'Why did you say that, Helen? Had you any reason, any real reason? Did you know something I didn't?'

Helen gently removed the mug from Kate's unresisting fingers and set it down precisely on the table, making room for it among the squeezed tubes of paint and the jam jars full of brushes.

'Observation, love.' She looked up at Kate, her expression serious and compassionate. 'I'm an artist, I look at people in a different way. I paint what I see, not only with these,' she gestured at her own eyes, 'but what

I see with something inside me, something which cuts through the top layer and lets what's inside show through. That's the way I look at you, the way I look at everything and everybody, the way I looked at Shirley—and believe me, love, there were times when Shirley didn't bear looking at.' She drew a deep breath and plunged her hands into the pockets of her oversized cardigan. 'All right, I'm going to say it, and if you walk out through the door and never speak to me again, I'll just have to bear it. I don't have anything concrete, Shirley chattered, but never about anything important. Didn't you ever notice that? But I couldn't ever forgive what she did to you, what she made you do so that she could be comfortable while she was with you.'

'Did you know she was going back to Theo?' Kate asked the question painfully.

'It was obvious, wasn't it?' Helen shrugged. 'Be honest, Kate. Could you see Shirley chucking all that money away? Your little sister was a conniving little so-and-so. She used you—but then I can't blame her. She'd always used you, and you were always willing to be used.'

Kate's smile was a travesty of the real thing. 'Yes, I was always willing, wasn't I?'

'And are you going to walk out of the door and never speak to me again?'

Kate shook her head. 'Never that, Helen. I wonder if you understand? It's been one hell of a shock and I still can't really believe it. It's going to take some time to get things in perspective again.'

'Love, for my advice, go back to your husband. Tell him about it, I'm sure he'll help.'

'You don't understand.' Kate hovered on the verge of hysterical laugher. 'Tell him? He told me and I still can't really believe it.'

Jerome came at six promptly and Helen let him in

and led him to the studio. Kate was still sitting in the velvet chair and he came to take her hand.

'Take her home,' advised Helen, 'get her to bed and give her something to make her sleep. She's all at sixes and sevens.'

'I think not.' Jerome pulled Kate to her feet. 'Kate has had some small shocks, but she's young and healthy, she'll soon get over them. Goodbye, Helen, Kate will write.' And without any fuss, he took Kate down to the street where Tobias was waiting with the car. 'There's another shock in store for you tomorrow.' He was quite cheerful as he helped her into the car and took the seat beside her.

She was woken by Mrs Davies at seven the next morning with a cup of tea and instructions to 'hurry, please, madam. Mr Jerome wants to leave within the hour.' Kate yawned and hoisted herself in the bed, fighting back an almost overmastering desire to go back to sleep.

'I'll have to pack my things,' she muttered as she gazed owlishly at the housekeeper.

'No need for that,' Mrs Davies pushed back the curtains. 'Mr Jerome tells me that you're not going back until tomorrow.'

'Then what's all the rush?' Kate felt herself growing stubborn and deliberately lingered over a bath and dressing before going slowly downstairs and helping herself to coffee from the pot on the breakfast table.

'If we're not going back to Derbyshire today, what's all the panic about?' she demanded mutinously. 'I was having a lovely sleep and I don't see why I have to be woken at the crack of dawn. The shops don't open till nine.'

'We aren't going shopping.' It was said absent-mindedly as if his mind was on other things, and he

watched her butter a slice of toast with a patient resignation. 'Hurry, please, there are some things that wait
for no man.'

'I want to know where we're going.' Kate was growing
belligerent. 'I may not be properly dressed.'

Jerome's eyes slid over her dark green trouser suit,
lingered for a moment on her flat, sensible shoes and
then came back to her face. 'You'll do, bring a jacket or
a coat.'

Nearly two hours later he pulled the car into a small
boatyard and hailed a man busy varnishing something
which looked like a mast.

Kate heard the faint, returning shout. 'Go on down,
sir. She's waiting for you.' Then she was hauled from
the car and practically frogmarched down a pebbly path
and out on to a small jetty.

'I'm not going a step farther until I know where we're
going and what you're up to,' she protested as her eyes
took in the seemingly never-ending expanse of water,
the white-capped waves and the little boat lying alongside the jetty and bobbing up and down in a very sick-
ening way.

The hand on her arm didn't slacken as she was forced
nearer to the boat. 'I'm sure Shirley must have told you
about this,' he was bland, 'my private yacht. She didn't
ever see it for herself, but that didn't stop her talking
about it. Wasn't I supposed to conduct amorous affaires
aboard it under the light of a Mediterranean moon?
Now, come and see for yourself.' He pushed her along a
swaying gangplank and on to the heaving deck, and
Kate took a moment to look around her.

She wouldn't have called this a yacht, to her a yacht
was white and slim with a high prow which cut through
the waves and with sufficient deck space for somebody
to sunbathe and perhaps an awning for when the sun

grew too hot. This boat didn't come into that category. It wasn't new, it wasn't particularly graceful, there was no beautiful rake to the bows and there wasn't room on the deck for a midget to sunbathe. She had little time to see more, because the hand about her arm was forcing her through a hatchway and down a steep companion into a small cabin.

'Satisfied?' he queried sardonically. 'These are the palatial quarters available—just the spot for erotic nights, don't you agree? Here,' he delved into a cupboard under a bunk, 'here are the silk sheets,' he tossed a dark blue, very hairy blanket at her 'and the galley is through there.'

'You didn't have to do this,' Kate looked at him angrily, 'and I wish you'd told me anyway, because there's something I think you should know. I get seasick stepping over a puddle!' And with great dignity she rose from her seat on the bunk, stepped past him, climbed the companion and made her way up the gangway to the beautiful steadiness of the stone wharf.

'That was a wasted morning,' she told him severely as they sat eating lunch in a pub near Maidstone. She attacked her steak with appetite and chewed reflectively. 'I don't understand why you did it.'

'Did what?'

'Wasted a day.' She stole a look at him from under her lashes. 'You've acted out of character.'

'Mmm?' There was a slight query in the sound, but his eyes were hooded and his face was enigmatic.

'Haring off like that,' she moved her slim shoulders restlessly and her fingers busied themselves rolling breadcrumbs into little balls on her plate. 'Down to the sea—where was it, by the way? I wasn't looking at signposts.'

'Near Romney.'

She nodded. 'It looked as though you did it impulsively, but you don't act on impulse. You plan and calculate. As I said before, it was out of character. Driving all that way to show me a boat! It doesn't make sense.'

'We're all human, Kate. Everyone does odd things sometimes.'

'Not you!' she was scornful. 'You're *not* human. You're one of those logic machines.'

'On the contrary,' his eyes slid over her with an expression of intense appreciation, 'I think there have been many times when you've found me very human indeed.'

The look in his eyes brought a swift, hot flush to her cheeks and she lowered her head and concentrated on her apple pie to hide her embarrassment. 'All the same,' she muttered, 'I don't understand it.'

'But understanding wasn't on my list,' Jerome pointed out gravely. 'I stipulated a loving, obedient wife. I didn't ask for understanding.'

At eight the next morning they left for Derbyshire. Eight o'clock—Jerome had been firm, he didn't want to get caught up in the commuter traffic and by starting fairly early they would be at his mother's house by lunchtime. Kate was striving to pretend that the past two days had never happened, and she hoped she was succeeding. As far as Jerome was concerned, they seemed to have made no difference, but for her, this couldn't be. She felt different inside and went to great pains to conceal it. Whether or not she was successful was impossible to say. She stole a glance at his profile and sighed.

'Sighing, Kate? Would you have preferred to stay in London?' He didn't take his eyes from the road.

'No, of course not.' For something to do, she rooted around in her bag. 'I want to get back to Philip as soon as possible and I thought you said that you had another visit to the States lined up. It will be much nicer at your mother's. I shan't feel so much like a prisoner.'

'Do I make you feel like a prisoner?' He sounded surprised.

'What else would I feel like? I've got a mental list of do's and don'ts a mile long. It's the nice thing about your mother. When you're not there to lay down the law, I have her as a jailer, and she's much more elastic than you are.' And pinning a smile of what she hoped was content on her face, she sat back in her seat and gave all her attention to the passing countryside.

CHAPTER NINE

THE weather was still cold, and here in Buxton it felt even colder. Kate had come in her old Morris 1000 and the heater was not as efficient as in the car's younger days. It was the one thing which Jerome's garage hadn't improved. Kate had dithered with excitement when the telephone call came. Her car was ready for collection or—the man's voice at the other end of the wire had been most obsequious—it could be delivered anywhere that Mrs Manfred wished. Mrs Jerome Manfred had wished it to be delivered to her in Derbyshire. She said so, rather hesitantly, and had been reduced to near silence by the very matter-of-fact 'Tomorrow, Mrs Manfred. Will that be convenient?'

Whoever it was had been assured that it would be *most* convenient, and she had found the car on the drive when she had come back from a walk with Philip and they had examined it carefully. It looked just like new. The rusting bits had been removed and someone had given it a complete respray which would have done credit to a Rolls-Royce. The seats had been either replaced or re-upholstered and the carpets had been renewed. A peep under the bonnet disclosed what looked like a new engine and Kate, seeing the keys still swinging in the ignition lock, had been tempted to try it out; not anywhere far, not with Philip with her, just up and down the drive a few times. All the squeaks and rattles had disappeared, it was just a matter of the heater, but that only meant wearing a warm coat, boots and gloves; it wasn't important.

Jerome had been with them over Easter, but now he

was away again for a few days and Kate had determined to try out her car on a long drive. Mrs Manfred thought this a splendid idea.

'Nanny and I are going to Matlock, we'll take Philip with us. Why don't you have an afternoon off?'

'Jerome said. . . .' Kate demurred.

'Just Jerome being over-careful,' his mother waved it aside airily. 'He always was a very responsible little boy. You'll be quite all right, won't you? You're not going to try to cross the Gobi Desert, just have a little run round. You can go to Eyam, that's the place where they quarantined themselves during the Plague, then you could go on through to Buxton and come back via Peverill Castle along the High Peak road. You'll enjoy it. Don't pick up any hitch-hikers, though.'

Despite her sheepskin coat and knee-length fur-lined boots, Kate shivered as she opened the car door in the car park at Buxton and then remembered a welcoming-looking café which she had passed on her way to the car park. She would go and get herself a nice cup of tea and possibly a bun, lunch had been a long time ago and she was beginning to feel hungry. She glanced at her watch and frowned! there wasn't a lot of time, not if she wanted to get back before lighting up time, so she locked up the little car and pulling on her sheepskin mitts, marched back along the street to the café.

It was pleasantly warm inside and Kate took a seat by the window where she could look out on the passers by. The tea, when it came, was hot and refreshing and the toasted teacakes looked and smelled delicious, golden brown and dripping with butter. She shrugged herself out of her sheepskin coat and sat back to enjoy herself. Somehow she had the feeling of being very wicked and her lips curved in an involuntary smile as she thought of what Jerome would say if he could see her now—but he couldn't. He was off somewhere—London, she thought, although she wasn't sure. He rang each evening, and when he rang this evening she would tell him what she'd been up to and he could make what he liked of it!

She poured herself another cup of tea and looked with regret at the empty teacake plate, wondering if she should be greedy and order some more, when her attention was attracted to a lone hiker—possibly, she thought, because the red knitted cap the man was wearing contrasted so violently with his red hair. Overlong hair which curled a bit on the collar of his nylon jacket. Her eyes left him, sliding across to two young girls in jeans and anoraks who were coming the other way, and then with a feeling of dismay she turned back to the hiker, taking in the short, rather thick neck, the wide shoulders, barrel chest and the confident walk. He paused to adjust his small pack and Kate went rigid. What on earth was Gerald doing up here? At almost the same moment he looked into the café window and saw her sitting there. He didn't smile or even look pleased to see her, but started moving towards the door with his 'dedicated' look on his face.

There was nowhere for her to hide and it was impossible for her to run, so she sat quite still on her chair, her teacup raised halfway to her lips. She heard the tinkle of the door bell which notified the proprietor of another customer and then came the slam of the door. Kate waited, motionless, schooling her face to a polite mask.

'Kate!' Gerald had taken off his pack and he flung himself into the chair opposite her. 'God, I thought I'd never see you again!'

'Hullo, Gerald.' Kate kept it cool. 'What are you doing up here?'

'It's the Easter vac.' He turned to order tea from the young girl who came to the table and turned back to Kate. 'I had an invitation from a friend, someone I met in London and who lives up here, and I thought, Why not? There was just a chance I might run into you, although I half expected you to be swanning around on the Riviera.' There was a pause while the girl brought his tea and arranged it before him. Kate watched him inspect the contents of the pot and the hot water jug before he poured. 'I saw Helen a couple of days ago,' he continued as he stirred his tea. 'She said you were living somewhere in Kensington, but when I tried to ring, the number was ex-directory.'

Kate nodded slightly. Jerome's telephone number would be ex-directory, especially to Gerald! She wanted to tell him to go, go back to London, that there was nothing for him here, and she hunted around for a way to say it. 'I hope you didn't come up here just to see me,' she said.

'That was the general idea.' He looked mysterious. 'My friend did say that the Jerome Manfreds were in residence.'

Kate gave a soft laugh. 'You make it sound quite feudal, but it's nothing of the kind. We're up here staying with his mother while the house in Kensington is finished. As soon as it's done, we'll be going back to London.' She drew a tiny breath and plunged. 'I wish we hadn't met, that you hadn't come up here.'

'Oh!' He grinned at her blithely. 'You mean the long arm of the Manfreds. Don't be an idiot, Kate. They don't frighten me.'

'Then you're stupid,' she snapped out the words, biting each one off sharply. 'In your position, I'd be shaking in my shoes. Jerome told me once, before we were married, that if I let you rescue me he'd destroy you.' Her mouth tightened. 'He doesn't make idle threats, Gerald, or say he'll do something if he can't do it. I'm not just thinking about you either, there's Philip to be considered—I don't want to be parted from him. You've been a good friend and I was very fond of you and I wouldn't like to see you hurt, but that's all. If you're walking, walk, but don't walk in my direction. You won't, not if you have any sense.'

Gerald's blue eyes went hard and his mouth twisted. 'Oh, I see!' He looked at her as if she was some low form of life. 'What I heard, then, is true?'

She raised her eyebrows. 'What you heard? What do you mean by that?'

'Just that you've found yourself a cosy little nest, well padded against inflation, and you're hanging on to it. I didn't believe it, not when I first heard it, but I'm beginning to believe it now. Not that I blame you. You've got just the one marketable commodity.' His eyes ran over her, taking in the soft tweed of her suit, the silk blouse and the slender but rounded figure beneath them. 'You got a good price for it, didn't you?' He was almost sneering at her.

'And would you have me now, Gerald, would you be willing to take me now? Another man's leavings—I don't think you'd like that!'

'No,' it came out violently. 'Not now I know what you are. I wouldn't have you as a gift. You sold yourself for a healthy bank balance and you're revelling in it.'

'For Philip,' she corrected him quietly. 'We had all this out before, before I married Jerome, before I even met him. Before I went to the cottage.'

'But Philip wasn't the only reason, was he, Kate?

Manfred had something else on you, something you didn't tell me about, something you didn't tell anybody, not even Helen. Shirley gave me a hint about it once, but I didn't believe her. Those were the days when I wouldn't have a word said against you, but it's different now. You've certainly opened my eyes. I actually thought you were decent!' Gerald kept his voice low so that to the other customers in the café it looked like a couple of friends having a pleasant chat, and Kate carefully kept her polite expression going, although she wanted to rush out into the clean air, away from the things he was saying.

'And what about Philip now?' he was asking. 'I hear you don't have so much to do with him any more. It didn't take long for you to install a nanny, did it? Where's it gone, your single-minded devotion to the boy? You were going to bring him up yourself, weren't you? You soon took advantage of a bottomless purse. It always amazes me how corruptible people are, even you, Kate. Somebody waves a cheque book under your nose and hey presto! you've developed a mind like a cash register, every basic ideal is thrown out of the window and you start enjoying being pampered. Well, make the most of it. You've become used to luxury, so my advice is, enjoy it while you can. You'll be out on your ear when Manfred gets tired of you, but you can always sell that body of yours again, can't you? Of course, it won't bring such a high price the next time or the time after that, will it? Second and third hand goods never do.'

Quietly and with as much dignity as possible, Kate rose to her feet, shrugging on her coat, pulling on her mitts and collecting her handbag.

'Goodbye, Gerald,' she made it calm and definite. 'I don't think we have anything more to say to each other.

You were a good friend when I needed one and I'll always remember you for that, but the rest, what you've just said is quite unforgivable,' and she walked steadily to the door, pausing on the way at the desk to pay the bill.

It was quite dark when she pulled into the drive and stopped the engine. She was too weary and disheartened to bother about garaging the little car, it had been an effort even to drive it back because all the way she had been haunted and pursued by the memory of Gerald's eyes as she had last seen them. Bright blue eyes, glittering and vindictive with a contempt in them which he had not even bothered to hide.

There had been something else as well, but she couldn't put a finger on it, a familiarity of expression which made her feel cheap and contemptible, and his words—there had been the same familiarity about them, as though she had heard them or something very like them before. She frowned with the effort of trying to remember and then gave it up. It was very hard to part from someone whom she had considered to be a friend, especially like this, and her slim shoulders drooped a little as she entered the house.

Hattie greeted her in the hall. Mrs Manfred was off down to Matlock with her dramatics, Master Philip was asleep and Nanny was in the small sitting room watching telly, and did she want anything to eat?

Kate smiled at the sour face and shook her head. 'I've been eating too much, Hattie.' It was only a gaunt, bad-tempered look which Hattie had. She was really a darling and completely happy as long as everybody was permanently stuffing themselves with her mouthwatering hams and meats, pies, tarts and cakes. 'I'm a bit tired,' she added as an excuse, 'and I stopped in Buxton and made a pig of myself on toasted teacakes. It's a long time since I've driven as far as I have today and coming back in the half dark——' she gave a delicate shudder. 'I think I'll go straight upstairs, have a hot bath and a very early night. Will you explain to Mrs Manfred for me?'

'That I will,' Hattie was sturdily positive. 'But there, I haven't known you all that long, but I reckon I know you well enough by now. You'll be down foraging for food halfway through the night, I'll take a bet on it. No wonder the modern generation gets indigestion, eating at all hours.' She stopped suddenly, noticing the weary droop of Kate's shoulders. 'Off upstairs with you and have your bath, I'll leave a nice dish of something in the larder for you, some chicken and ham, eh? Eating too much! Don't expect me to believe that or that you're worried about your weight. A good belly makes a good back, that's what I always say!'

The bath was relaxing, and after it Kate practically fell into bed. She didn't think she'd sleep much, her mind was too active. First she had to tell Jerome. Not everything, of course, certainly not Gerald's bitter, spiteful remarks, just that she'd seen him, a chance encounter. She fell to wondering where Jerome was and if he would ring tonight. If he did, his mother would answer it, and she wondered if he would ask for her. The familiar hot feeling uncoiled inside her. She wanted him, she wanted him desperately, and she stared into the darkness with wide, shamed eyes.

It was just as Hattie had predicted. In the darkness, much later, Kate stirred and woke, filled not with love but with a ravening hunger. She switched on the bed-side lamp and consulted the clock—two a.m. Closing her eyes, she snuggled down, pulling the pillow under her cheek, trying to find oblivion once again in sleep, but a vision of Hattie's promised dish of chicken and ham swam before her closed eyes and her stomach gave a protesting rumble.

With a little sigh she reached towards the end of the bed for her dressing-gown and pushed her feet into her slippers before making her way through the sleeping house and down to the kitchen.

Kate had cleared the last morsel from her plate and was busy making herself a cup of tea when she heard the click of the front door and then felt the draught as the kitchen door opened. She stood quietly by the counter, the teapot in her hand. It wasn't necessary to turn around, she knew who had come in. With despair, she continued looking at the red roses on the teapot without really seeing them. This was what being in love had done for her! If she had been blind, deaf and dumb and had her nose stopped up with cotton wool, she would know when Jerome came into the the room. She could feel it on her skin, and feel also the traitorous warmth uncoiling itself from her stomach and spreading through her body.

Without turning her head, she asked, 'Will you have tea or would you prefer coffee?'

'Tea, I think, Kate.' He sounded rather tired and she lifted down another cup and saucer before she turned to look at him. He looked tired, and she crushed down a violent impulse which bade her go and draw his head down on to her breast while she smoothed away the hard lines from around his mouth with a gentle finger. It all hurt so much that she was breathless with the pain. Instead, she warmed the teapot, added tea, fetched milk from the fridge and clattered in the cutlery drawer for teaspoons.

'Would you like something to eat?' she burbled. 'Hattie's left some chicken and ham, it's all ready and it's very good. I've just had some.'

'Mmm.' It was a contented sound, and she whisked herself off to the larder, the wide skirts of her dressing gown flying about her slippered feet.

When Jerome had eaten, she poured him another cup of tea and then sat quietly, waiting for him to speak. She watched as he leant back in the chair with a sigh of relief and lit a cigarette.

'Any news?'

'Lots,' she smiled widely. 'Tammy has had her litter, four of them, three dogs and one little bitch, and your mother's over the moon. She says one of the dogs is going to be a winner, although how she can tell, I don't know—they all look alike to me. Oh, and the breach between Hattie and Nanny has been healed.'

'How did that happen?' Jerome looked rather amused. 'They've been engaged in a cold war ever since Nanny arrived.'

'Camphor.' Kate was succinct. 'Philip came down one morning smelling to high heaven and I found this little flannel bag round his neck. Nanny explained it to me and I was saying something about old wives' tales when Hattie came leaping to her defence. Nanny was quite pink and Hattie was bristling. Apparently Hattie's grandma wore a camphor bag around *her* neck until the day she died and never suffered with her chest. Hattie's even supplied the flannel for several more bags, and now Philip is going about smelling like a gigantic mothball, but he's stopped wheezing. It's the vapours.' Kate's eyes were shining with mirth. 'They clear the tubes!' Abruptly she changed the subject. 'Where have you been this time?'

'Brussels first and then Paris. Very tiring, especially Brussels. It's being said that Brussels manufactures red tape, there's so much of it in the Common Market. Anything else?'

'Yes,' she nodded. 'Thank you for my car. The garage rang and asked where I wanted it and I said "here" and lo, it came.'

'Mmm. I saw it on the drive, I nearly went into it in the dark. You should put it in the garage.'

'I've been out in it,' she was a trifle defiant. 'Alone—I didn't take Philip or Nanny with me. I went to Buxton.'

Jerome reached for another cigarette and the thought came to Kate that perhaps he was smoking too much. He looked at her over the flame of his lighter. 'And?' he prompted.

'I saw Gerald,' she said baldly. 'It was quite un-expected—one of those accidental things. He's walking up here during the Easter vac.'

'An odd coincidence. . . .' He spared a glance for her face, his grey eyes unfathomable in their fringes of dark lashes.

'In a way, I suppose,' Kate shrugged, and steadied herself. 'He said a friend, someone he'd met in London, a friend who lives up here somewhere had invited him. He was hoping to run into me, he said.'

'And he did!'

'Mmm. I was in a café, having tea and looking out of the window. He came along the road and looked in and saw me. He came in and we talked for a while, that's all. I didn't try to escape,' she said gravely.

'And it wasn't very pleasant?'

'How did you know that?' Her green eyes widened in surprise.

'Your face, Kate. Usually, it's calm and serene, especially when you think somebody's watching you. Just now, there was a twist of distaste about your mouth. Gerald was unpleasant, I gather.'

'Very unpleasant,' she said fiercely, and her eyes glittered. 'He has a very poor opinion of me now. He thinks

I've been corrupted by a life of idleness and too much money. He was sitting at my table. I left him sitting there.'

'I see. You sold yourself for a bottomless bank balance, is that it?'

'Something like,' Kate muttered almost to herself. 'It was unjustified!' Her eyes sparkled with indignation. 'I'm just the same as I always was. And now, if you don't mind, I'm trying to forget about it so I'd rather not be reminded.'

'A lesson learned, Kate?' He raised a dark eyebrow sardonically. 'It couldn't have happened if you'd had somebody with you, if you'd taken Nanny and Philip or my mother.'

That was a thought she didn't care for, it made her feel vaguely guilty, so she switched to another facet of the subject. 'I wonder who this friend is, the one he's staying with? I've never heard him mention anybody from this part of the country before.'

'Who knows?' Jerome glanced at his watch. 'Come to bed, Kate, it's getting cold in this kitchen. Hattie switches the heat off at night—like you, she has a saving disposition, almost cheeseparing!' With an arm about her he drew her up the stairs and as the bedroom door closed behind them, he held her quietly while his hands smoothed away her dressing gown and then her night-dress. She stood in his arms, a slim, curved, pale column in the fugitive moonlight, quite still and waiting.

'So you're just the same as you always were?' He murmured the words against the skin of her neck and into the curve of her shoulder. 'You haven't changed at all, Kate?' And she thought he was laughing as his lips found her eager mouth.

Kate slept only for a few hours. She woke at six and in the pale light turned to examine her sleeping husband.

She liked looking at him when he was asleep for at least two reasons. He didn't know she was examining him, so she didn't have to be shy or discreet about it. She didn't have to school her face or hide her eyes, and her mouth could be as soft and tender as she liked. Secondly, as she had noted before, he looked a lot younger and even a bit vulnerable when he was sleeping. It was a pity he had to lose that look when he woke up, she infinitely preferred him without his veneer of hard, glossy, worldly-wise sophistication.

And what was she going to do about loving him? Nothing! She couldn't stop, it had crept up on her quietly without her noticing and now it was part of her. To stop now would be like cutting off her hands or tearing her heart out. She wouldn't be complete any longer.

She gave a little rueful smile. She wasn't at the 'I'll lie down and let you walk all over me' stage, she very much doubted if she ever would be, but she was pretty near it. It made of her life a hell which she wouldn't have changed for any heaven that didn't contain Jerome. And she still didn't know how long it would last! Reluctantly she dragged her eyes away from their rapt contemplation and huddling herself into her dressing-gown and gathering up an armful of fresh clothing, she went off to the bathroom.

When she returned to the bedroom Jerome was still sleeping, so she tiptoed out and down to the kitchen where Hattie was energetically beating up her scrambled egg mixture. She spared Kate a sour glance.

'Early bird this morning! What's wrong, aren't you well?'

'Yes, I'm quite well, thank you.' Kate's eyes twinkled. 'What did you think might be the matter with me?'

'Morning sickness!' Hattie gave her a cynical look.

'It's what usually gets young wives up an hour before time.'

Kate shook her head mournfully. 'I'm sorry to disappoint you, Hattie, but no!'

Hattie sniffed. 'You aren't disappointing me,' she snorted. 'It's the missus you're disappointing. Well, if you're not ill, what do you want in my kitchen at this hour of the morning?'

'Advice.' Kate put on a slightly worried look. 'Jerome came in at two this morning. I gave him some of your ham and chicken thing and a cup of tea before he went to bed. Now he's still asleep, and he never sleeps after seven o'clock. Do you think I should wake him, take him up a cup of coffee or something?'

'Leave him till eight, you can take him some coffee then.' The old lady's voice harshened. 'Don't stand there dithering in the doorway. There's a pot of tea made and if you want some, come in, shut that door and sit at the table. I can't stand people havering about.' Briskly, she poured the tea, sparing Kate a searching glance. 'All smiles now you've got your man back, aren't you? Well, don't think to get round me with your soft ways, because you won't do it! Do you want a piece of toast with your tea?'

Kate sat on the side of the bed giggling, as she retailed parts, but only parts, of this conversation to Jerome while she watched him drink the coffee she had carried upstairs.

'A friend for life,' he gave it as a serious judgment. 'You'll be able to turn her round your little finger.'

Kate wanted to wail at him, 'Why can't I do it with you?' but instead she asked sedately how long he was here for.

'Three days,' he was bland. 'I've given myself three days' holiday, then I have another visit to the States.

After that, things should be fairly quiet for a while.'

Kate removed herself from the side of the bed and picked up the empty coffee cup and saucer. 'Mmm, I'm glad of that. A few more of these hectic weeks and you'll be suffering from jet lag.'

Jerome raised himself once more to a sitting position. 'Kate,' he sounded surprised, 'you're becoming wifely!'

'Is it a bad habit?' she queried from the doorway. 'Not to worry, though, unlike distemper, it isn't catching!'

Philip hailed the advent of his uncle, after such a short absence, with noisy enthusiasm and promptly started misbehaving. Despite Kate's protests that he was only a little excited, Jerome banished him to the nursery, from where his roars of disappointment could have been heard in the next county.

'Our nephew has a healthy pair of lungs.' Jerome was unmoved by the noise and blandly escorted Kate out to the little Morris. 'Get in!'

Kate hesitated. From the window of the nursery, Philip could be heard at full volume. '*My* go for a ride! *My* go in car!' He was having a little difficulty with his pronouns, but he was making his wishes abundantly clear.

'Couldn't we take him . . .?' she voiced the suggestion hesitantly. 'He's only a little boy. . . .'

'No, we can't,' Jerome was firm. 'He has to learn that he can't have everything his own way.'

'He doesn't,' she protested. 'He doesn't have everything his own way.' She stood by the little car, the pale sun shining on her chestnut hair and her mouth set in an obstinate line. 'He's very good ordinarily, it's just that he wants. . . .'

'Precisely.' Jerome was also obstinate and he cut

through her plea in a hardhearted fashion. 'He wants!' He cocked his head to indicate the roars of temper coming from the window. 'I suppose you and my mother, not to mention Hattie as well, have been spoiling him to death. No wonder Nanny's having trouble with him!'

'That's not true,' Kate said fiercely. 'We don't spoil him, we love him. Every child needs love. I don't suppose you went short of it when you were Philip's age. You were probably just as much of a pest at times as Philip is.'

Her remarks bounced off his indifference and he merely told her to get in the car. 'In the driving seat, please. I want to see what sort of a driver you are.'

She settled herself behind the wheel and glared at him. 'I've been driving for six years,' she said between gritted teeth. '*And* I passed my test first time. I'm perfectly competent and I don't need you to tell me whether I can drive or not!'

'Drive, Kate.' He was implacable.

The demonstration of her driving ability was not a success and to be honest, Kate had to admit to herself that, had she been an examiner, testing herself, she would have failed herself without any doubt. For some stupid reason Jerome's very presence in the passenger seat made her nervous. He didn't say a word or even look at her, but she could feel waves of disapproval coming from him and hitting her as she missed gears, went too fast or too slow and made an apalling mess of at least one road junction. They had covered about fifteen miles before he told her to pull in to the car park of a country pub.

'We'll have lunch here,' he decreed, and with a hand firm about her elbow, he led her to the bar.

'Not a very good demonstration,' was his comment

as they sat at the dining table, and Kate found herself wondering how she could ever have thought she loved him. No woman in her right mind could love this arrogant, scathing monster, this ultimate in male chauvinism. She didn't love him at all, she hated him! He was insensitive, he didn't have an ounce of understanding or human compassion and she wished she'd never seen him. She had a wild desire to get up, stalk out and drive away, leaving him stranded here, but she stifled the desire almost as soon as it was born. It wouldn't do any good. He would probably take the little car away from her, and she didn't want that.

'We can't all be perfect,' she smiled sweetly. 'I'm not usually as bad as I was this morning, but, to be candid, I find you a bit off-putting.' And she turned her attention to her lunch, devouring fried scampi and afterwards pineapple fritters with an unimpaired appetite while he talked casually about the weather, the political situation and other boring subjects. Gradually she found herself relaxing and by the time she had finished her coffee, she was quite good-tempered again so that she was able to get into the little car and drive it back calmly and competently, without being a danger to other road users.

'Much better,' he gave her a brief smile as she drove into the garage and switched off the ignition.

'And may I drive it?' It took a great deal of self-control to get the required submissive note into her voice, but she did it.

'Mmm,' he leaned across and kissed her so that her heart started to bang like a drum. 'It was much better that time. Your trouble, Kate, is that you tend to become too emotional. It wasn't me that made you so bad when we started out, it was your bit of temper because you couldn't have your own way about Philip. You can't concentrate on driving when you're like that. You need a cool head and a quiet mind. But yes, you can drive, but not alone. please. You can take Mother with you, she likes jauntering about and she won't distract you as Philip would.' He sounded so infernally priggish that she forgot how pleasant the kiss had been, how much she had wanted it to go on and on.

As she came round to the front of the house, her eyes fell on the red sports car parked by the door and she gave an inward squeal of rage. Estelle was here, and she would stay to tea and quite possibly dinner as well. Kate masked her disappointment beneath a bright and sparkling smile. Jerome was only here for three days and one of those days was nearly gone already. She didn't want to share him with the black-haired, passionate wench, but the wench would stick like glue and she knew it! Estelle would stay on and on and on, she would have to be practically thrown out, and all the time she would be making her sweet little nasty remarks and ruining everything.

'Oh, look!' Kate maintained her bright smile. 'Your girl-friend's called. Isn't that nice! I do hope she stays for tea.' She looked up and surprised a faint smile on his face.

'*Not* my girl-friend, Kate, and you know it!' he drawled. 'I've no time to spare for girl-friends. I've got my hands full at present trying to satisfy a very demanding wife!'

CHAPTER TEN

KATE squealed with ill-concealed irritation and for one moment was tempted to throw the hairdryer on the floor. The only thing which stopped her was the knowledge that it wasn't her hairdryer. Had it been hers, she would not only have thrown it on the floor, she would have changed her soft slippers for a pair of cloggy mules and jumped on it! But the hairdryer was on loan from little Dodie and, as with the vacuum cleaner, in Dodie's hands it probably worked. In Kate's, it did not. For nearly half an hour she had been sitting here in the bedroom, trying to dry the heavy hank of wet hair which hung down her back, and all she had achieved so far was a tremendous blast of cold air. There was no heat to be had in the thing.

Kate moved her slender shoulders irritably and shivered. Perhaps she'd got the setting wrong. She pointed the business end of the dryer away from her and examined the switch. The little red arrow pointed firmly to HOT; maybe it didn't work on this setting, so she switched it to WARM and held a tentative hand in the blast. Nothing happened, the blast was as strong as ever, but the temperature did not rise by one degree. She switched to COLD; again there was no change, and then she tried OFF and the blast died away. She didn't know why she was bothering, she had already tried all these things and it was becoming increasingly evident that whatever worked the heating had died on her.

Kate had one last try with the dryer, shivering in the icy blast as it struck her damp head. That head was beginning to feel like the tip of an iceberg and the remainder of her body was cooling rapidly. There was only one thing to do, go down to the kitchen, open all the dampers of the solid fuel cooker and the oven door and try to dry her hair there.

Kate gazed down at herself. She was wearing her old dressing gown over her undies and a pair of scuffed slippers on her feet. Not the ideal wear for kneeling on a rug with her head halfway up a chimney, but fortunately there was nobody to see her and there wouldn't be for the rest of the afternoon.

Jerome was in New York. He hadn't asked her to go along with him this time and she had been hurt about it. She wouldn't have gone even if he had asked her, but all the same, it would have been nice to be asked. Jerome's mother, together with Nanny and Philip, had gone to spend the afternoon in Matlock, mainly to re-plenish Nanny's diminishing hoard of knitting wool; Hattie had taken the early bus to Calver where she was visiting an aged aunt and little Dodie had gone home yesterday, sick with a gumboil which was distorting one side of her face until it looked like some overripe fruit, red and shiny and threatening to burst. Dodie was now in her bed and suffering the injections of antibiotics with the same stoic fatalism as she had suffered her gumboil, so Kate had the house to herself.

Carefully, she restored the hairdryer to its box while she made plans. She would go down to the kitchen and her first task would be to open the dampers and get the fire pulled up red from Hattie's carefully banked-down condition. Then she would make herself a cup of good, strong, hot tea, and only after she had drunk it would she kneel down in front of the cooker and get her hair dry and, with any luck, get warm again.

Soundlessly, she fled down the stairs, and stopped dead on the last one as she heard the sound. It was like

a banging followed by a cracking sound. Hattie must
have returned early. Kate looked at her watch and dismissed that idea. It couldn't be that. Hattie would only
now be reaching Calver, so it wasn't Hattie, and the
noise wasn't coming from the kitchen anyway. It seemed
to be coming from nearer at hand. Kate waited a couple
of seconds and the noise came again, from the study. She
went rigid.

There was only one explanation that she could think of:
burglars! And she wasn't dressed to receive burglars,
and it was too late for her to run back upstairs and
change into slacks and a jumper. Her mind ran over the
possibilities. The traditional weapon to repel burglars
was, without doubt, a good stout poker; it was equally
useful against housebreakers too. There was a difference
between housebreakers and burglars, she remembered,
although she couldn't quite remember what; she thought
it had something to do with the time of day. Anyway,
what she wanted was a poker, and she didn't have one
handy. The nearest was the long, polished brass one in
the kitchen, and to get it she would have to pass the
study door. If whoever was in there had posted a look-
out, she would be caught unarmed and defenceless.

Along the hall, near the front door, was a side table
with above it a big brass gong, and on the table lay the
hammer with its fat round head. Kate dismissed it. The
hammer was too short, less than a foot long, and the
felt head of it was squishy. For striking a gong, it was
ideal, but as a weapon, no! It would be like trying to hit
somebody with a spoonful of jelly. Her eyes slid farther
alone to the umbrella stand and she felt a glow of satisfaction. Not a poker but a walking stick! A good stout
blackthorn, well over three feet long, with a brass ferrule
and a large, heavy silver ball mounted at the top as a
handle.

Silently she tiptoed across the hall and drew the stick from its resting place. She tried a few experimental swipes with it and was quite pleased with her performance. She could either poke with the brass-tipped ferrule or bash with the ball. Either method would prove to the housebreaker that she was a force to be reckoned with!

There had been complete silence from the study for some moments, then, as she cautiously approached the door, the noise came again—groaning, protesting noise followed by a splintering crack and then a drawn-out squeak. Kate twisted the door knob fiercely and flung the door part open. Then, grasping her stick in both hands by the ferrule, she pushed her way through the part opened door. The sight which met her eyes stopped her dead in her tracks.

The room was in utter chaos. The filing cabinets along the wall had been wrenched open, the drawers pulled out and the floor was a litter of pedigree charts, bills, receipts, bank statements and accounts. Kate's head swung to the french windows and the old-fashioned desk. The windows were open and between them and the desk stood Estelle, a small, slim Estelle in narrow black trousers and a skinny polo-necked black sweater under a black leather jacket. The thought, unbidden, slipped through Kate's mind—just the gear for a break-in! The two girls stared at each other in speechless surprise for all of ten seconds. Estelle recovered first.

'Caught in the act!' Her laugh was high, brittle and a bit forced.

Kate advanced into the room, taking a firmer grip of her walking stick.

'What in hell do you think you're doing?'

'Naughty, naughty!' Estelle laughed again. 'Bad language, dear Kate. What does it look like? A little forced entry,' she indicated the french window, 'a little search,' her eyes flicked to the filing cabinets and then to the desk, 'and a spot of unlawful possession.' She held up a slim, brown manilla envelope. 'You're too late, Kate. I found what I came for and I've got it!' She smiled triumphantly, and leaned back against the wall, still within easy reach of the open window.

'I thought the house would be empty, I thought you'd gone with the others.' She smiled again, a not very nice smile. 'I watched the car going and I felt sure you'd be in it, but I was wrong, wasn't I? Never mind, I think I like it better this way. I've been wanting to see you squirm for a long time. Start squirming, Kate! You know what's in here, don't you?' and she waved the envelope. 'I haven't looked, but I know!'

'Who told you?' Kate was angry and it showed in her voice.

Estelle tittered. 'Nobody told me, darling. Nobody had to tell me anything! I worked it out for myself. A few hints from one direction, a couple of pointers from another, remembering something Theo once said about some naughty pictures, and then, the little bit your redheaded Gerald could tell me. It was easy! I knew what to look for and I knew where to look.'

'Gerald?' Kate's mouth tightened. 'What do you know about Gerald?'

'Quite a lot, darling!' Again came the high-pitched, excited laugh. 'I met him in London, while I was doing my own little bit of detective work. I knew he was going to be useful. It was easy, he's a sucker for a bit of flattery and wide-eyed innocence. I had him eating out of my hand in no time at all.'

'And he's staying with you now.' Kate nodded to herself in understanding and took a firmer grasp of her walking stick as she advanced on Estelle, a battle light glowing in her eyes. Estelle retreated a pace or two and stopped.

'Careful, darling,' she admonished in a high, triumphant voice. 'Try anything and I'll run and I won't run quietly. I'll scream bloody murder and as soon as I find someone to listen to me, I'll tell them I caught you ransacking this place, that I tried to stop you and that you attacked me.' She glanced down at the envelope and then up again at Kate, so very slyly. 'After all, darling, you've much more reason to want this than I have and more reason to want it kept quiet. Just think for a moment what will happen if I make a fuss. The police will take this,' she waved the envelope, 'they'll produce it in court as evidence—and that's curtains for you, darling!'

'I haven't touched anything!' Kate was indignant as she looked around at the mess.

'Neither have I!' Estelle held out her black-gloved hands in protesting innocence. 'I was only trying to stop you smashing up Mrs Manfred's home, wasn't I?'

Kate felt as though she was in the middle of some ghastly nightmare and there was no way out. Reluctantly, she let the head of the walking stick fall and stood leaning against it.

'That's better,' Estelle smiled her approval and became crisp. 'Here's what you do. Get upstairs and pack your little bag, then get into your old jalopy and go. At once! No hanging about to make tearful explanations. I want you out of here before Mrs Manfred gets back and I want you well away before Jerome returns, understand? You're to leave a note for Jerome, very short, just goodbye, and tell him to come across and see me at once. Tell him that I'll explain for you.'

'And if I don't?' Kate was playing for time while she thought. She could feel her courage returning, and that was a good thing. This girl was obviously out of her head, at least temporarily, and there was no use in arguing with her or trying to make her see reason.

'If you don't, I'll give this envelope to your redheaded ex-boy-friend—or could you call him a friend any longer? He doesn't feel very friendly towards you, in fact he's got a big case of the hates. He wants to see you squirm as well. He tells me he does a column for one of the London dailies, he should be able to make a juicy article out of what's in this envelope. Remember now— *out*! And as quickly as possible. Don't forget the note for Jerome. I want to see him as soon as he returns. You make sure he understands that!' And with a final triumphant glance over her shoulder, Estelle skipped lightly out through the french windows and sped along the drive to where her red sports car was parked.

Kate watched her go with relief and took a few minutes to try to conquer the trembling of her body induced by anger, fear and despair. She sagged in a chair breathing deeply and trying to get her thoughts into some semblance of order. All along, she told herself, she knew that the whole thing, the running away, the ridiculous marriage, all of it was a nasty mess, and from where she was sitting, it was looking even messier. Estelle wouldn't see reason, not if it was painted in foot high letters and held in front of her; she was obsessed with getting rid of Kate and she couldn't see farther than the end of her nose. And Gerald wouldn't want to see reason. He'd been waiting for something like this! He would take it and squeeze every last drop of beastliness out of it and into the column he wrote. Kate's head jerked up at the thought and her back straightened. Over her dead body would he do that! The first thing was to get in touch with Jerome, and to hell with Estelle and her commands!

Her eyes sought the carriage clock on the mantelpiece. She supposed it was lucky to be in an area which had escaped Estelle's depredations. The pendulum was swinging fussily and the hands pointed to half past four. New York time was five hours back, that meant it would be half past eleven there, half past eleven in the morning. Jerome would be at the office and with luck she would be able to catch him before lunch.

Her hands shook so much as she picked up the telephone that she had to put the handset on the table while she dialled the New York number and use two hands to do it, and she waited in an agony of suspense in case the international switchboard was blocked solid and she would have to wait and dial again. Luck was with her and she heard the ringing tone.

A girl's voice answered, very clear as if it was in the same room as herself. 'Manfred Corporation, New York office. Can I help you?'

'Mrs Jerome Manfred calling,' Kate was terse. 'I wish to speak with Mr Manfred.'

'One moment, please,' the slightly nasal voice sounded doubtful. 'I think that line is busy,' then the voice cheered up. 'No, Mrs Manfred, it's clear now. I'm putting you thrrrough!'

But it wasn't Jerome answering, it was the secretary, and she was full of sorrow. 'No, Mrs Manfred, Mr Manfred's not here. I obtained a cancellation for him on a late flight from Kennedy yesterday. He should be in London now.'

Overcome by disappointment, Kate thanked the girl and hung up. Then she dialled the London office, but once again she was disappointed. Mr Manfred hadn't been in and they weren't expecting him. A third call to the Kensington house elicited similar results. Mrs Davies hadn't seen him either, he certainly hadn't been there.

Kate felt like crying. He could be anywhere—Paris, Brussels, Rome, the list was endless and she didn't know any of the numbers to ring.

Well, she pulled herself together, the first thing to do was get dressed. Something warm, because she was shivering in earnest now and she felt cold all the way through. Her hair was still wet, but that didn't matter. She sped upstairs and began hastily assembling some garments on the bed—a pair of thick brown wool trousers, an equally thick brown wool jumper with a polo neck, a cardigan which matched, some thick tights and some short, fur-lined boots. She was just struggling to tie back her hair with a piece of ribbon and wondering if she'd have time for a cup of tea when she heard the sound of fat tyres on the gravel. Mrs Manfred's Rolls, and what was she to do now? She skipped over to the window and looked down on the drive. There was no sign of the Rolls, the car beneath the window shone a dull, metallic grey: Jerome's Ferrari!

Kate struggled back into her dressing gown, her cold fingers fumbling with the zip, and charged down the stairs, her heart beating violently.

Through the open door of the study she could see him, glaring around him with disapproval, and she had barely entered the room before she was storming at him.

'Where the hell have you been?' Fright made her voice shrill. 'I've been phoning everywhere for you. I phoned New York and you'd left, I phoned the London office and you hadn't even been there. I phoned Mrs Davies and you hadn't been there either. Why don't you let people know where you are, instead of vanishing off into the blue? It's most inconsiderate!' She was beginning to stutter with a mixture of fright, anger and tears. Drawing a deep breath, she tried to be calm, to steady herself. 'I've got to go,' she said desperately, 'and you mustn't try to stop me. You've got to go across and see Estelle, at once. Please do that, and do it now! She's been here this afternoon, while I was upstairs washing my hair. She's been through everything,' Kate gestured at the open drawers and the mess, 'and she's broken into your desk. Look!' She walked round the desk and noticed for the first time the jagged splinters where the locks had been forced and the drawers wrenched open. She touched the raw scars in the wood with a trembling finger. 'Estelle,' her voice shook, 'she's found that envelope, the one marked "Kate", the one with the negatives in it, and she's d-damaged the desk.'

Jerome stood silently watching her, and it was his silence and immobility which infuriated her. Tears sprang to her eyes and she dashed them away with the back of her hand. 'Why did you keep them?' she demanded. 'Why didn't you destroy them? Didn't you realise how dangerous they were? You might have known that one day they'd get into the wrong hands, things like that always do! Now Estelle's got them and she's going to use them.'

Angrily she rounded the desk and came to stand in front of him, her fists raised to batter against his chest, and she was crying in earnest now. 'Estelle says she won't do anything if we do as she says, but I don't trust her, she's got Gerald with her. That's where he's been staying, she's his "friend" whom he met in London.' Kate was battering Jerome's chest with futile fists. 'He'll have those negatives from her, I know he will! And he'll spread them through his nasty little column. Why did you marry me?' she moaned. 'Why didn't you just take Philip and leave me to stew in my own juice? Don't stand there grinning at me like a Cheshire cat, you great brute! Can't you see what's going to happen?'

Her fists stopped battering and she seized his arms and tried to shake him. 'Do you want me to spell it out in words of one syllable? All right, I will! I've told you, modelling's a short life and faces get forgotten very quickly. I've been out of the business for six months, I'm as dead as a dodo. When that column goes out, the name to the pictures won't be Kate Forrest, nobody knows her, and it won't be Noelle Lowe, nobody will remember her. The name will be Mrs Jerome Manfred. Jerome, don't you understand? They'll crucify you! You, not me! I wouldn't care if it was me. They can say what they like about me, I don't matter, but Gerald will make you a laughing stock. Millionaire financier taken in by a "girlie" model! And it'll be all my fault!' It came out as another moan. 'I should have let you take Philip, then this would never have happened. And it's your fault as well.' Her eyes glittered with more tears. 'You should have destroyed those negatives. You didn't need to keep them. I'd given my word, hadn't I? I might have wanted to break it, but I couldn't have done it.'

Jerome spoke for the first time. 'Stop it, Kate. Be quiet, you're becoming hysterical.' His finger came under her chin, tipping up her face. He looked down at her tear-drowned eyes and bent his head to kiss her trembling lips. 'There are no negatives,' he said matter-of-factly as he raised his head.

Kate went very still. 'What did you say?'

'I said there are no negatives.' He put his arms round her, drawing her close. 'I burned them, Kate. They weren't any good, not to me. I had to have the real thing.'

She looked up at him wonderingly. 'The real thing?' Her voice was a squeak.

'You, Kate!' He said it quietly and with hardly any emphasis, as if he was explaining something to a backward child, and Kate started to tremble uncontrollably.

'Bed, I think.' He caught her up swiftly and bore her upstairs. 'We'll get you warm first. Do you know that your hair's still wet? Then I'll get you a hot drink and we'll have a few explanations. One of us, and I think it's you, my dear, is on the wrong wavelength.'

He switched on the electric overblanket and swiftly and competently put her into the bed, stripping away her dressing gown and tossing it over the back of a chair. Then he went downstairs and reappeared a few minutes later with a cup of tea and a small quantity of brandy in a glass. Kate was still shuddering and he raised her and put the glass to her lips.

'Drink it up, Kate. I know you don't like it, but that doesn't matter. You've had a shock. Drink it!' And once again, as he had done at the cottage, he forced the glass against her lips until she gulped.

'Good,' he grinned at her. 'I thought I was going to have to hold your nose and pour it down your throat. Here, have your tea now, it'll take the taste away, and when you've stopped shaking, we'll. . . .' He stopped speaking with a muffled expletive and crossed to the window where he peered down at the drive. 'Mother's back,' he grimaced slightly. 'She's going to want a few explanations as well. I'll go down and get those over first.'

As he was passing the bed, Kate put out a hand to stop him. She didn't know why she was doing it—the brandy, she supposed. Alcohol was said to loosen the tongue! 'I love you,' she whispered, and lay watching him with agonised eyes.

'I know.' He bent over and kissed her gently. 'But it will have to wait. This is one time when Mother comes first.' And he went out swiftly, closing the door behind him.

Kate lay in a welter of emotions. She'd made a mess of it, she was certain. She shouldn't have said it, Jerome didn't want love, he didn't need it! He wanted her, she knew that. Only the night before he had gone to New York this last time, he had spent half the night proving to her that she was a desirable woman and that his desire for her had not diminished by one iota—but that wasn't love! He didn't love her. He took great care of her, but that wasn't love either. And now she had laid bare her heart. She smiled at such an old fashioned phrase and the smile was wiped off her face very quickly. Perhaps he was one of those men who aimed at total capitulation and once they'd got it, became bored and uninterested, one who lived for the battle and the victory and, when it was achieved, went looking for new conquests.

Kate buried her face in her pillow and gave up even trying to think. She just lay there in a puddle of misery until her mother-in-law came in, tiptoeing across the carpet with exaggerated caution.

'Brave girl, silly girl!' Mrs Manfred scolded softly. 'Why didn't you phone for the police? You shouldn't ever try to tackle housebreakers on your own, it's ridiculous and very unwise. You could have been badly injured, and there's nothing in the house worth that!'

So Jerome had a story about housebreakers? He hadn't mentioned Estelle or her part in the affair. Kate struggled up in bed. 'I didn't think about the phone,' she sighed wearily. 'I know I should have thought about it, but I became obsessed with finding a poker,' she giggled weakly. 'I was quite vexed that you didn't keep one in the hallway. All I could find was a walking stick and I was scared stiff when I pushed the door open.'

'You're very lucky to be all in one piece,' Mrs Manfred continued her scold. 'There's a lot of this house-breaking going on nowadays, there was the case of that young boy who disturbed a gang while he was delivering papers, do you remember? If it ever happens again, which God forbid, you're to phone the police, if you can get to the phone and then you must lock yourself in your room and pretend you're not there. Now Nanny's coming in to give you something to take away the shock, it'll make you feel drowsy for a while, but you're to take it. And Hattie shall bring your dinner up on a tray. We're all agreed, you're to stay in bed for the rest of the day.'

'I'm not an invalid,' Kate protested, but even as she protested, she could feel herself trembling still. 'I'm quite well, really I am. Just give me half an hour and I'll be downstairs for tea.' She didn't want to stay in the bedroom alone with only her thoughts for company. Those thoughts hurt too much and they were all of Jerome. Even Philip didn't have so much importance now! Now, he was just a little boy, a very lovable little boy whom she loved but not idolatrously. Yes, that was the word she wanted. Her love for Jerome bordered on the idolatrous, and she could only lie here thinking about it, wondering how long it would last and how she'd cope with a mistress when he became bored with her.

'Here she is,' Mrs Manfred became brisk. 'Have you got it, Nanny? Good!' Kate was presented with a glassful of milky fluid which tasted foul and Nanny stroked her forehead, plumped up her pillows and pressed her back on them firmly.

'We'll be as right as rain by tomorrow morning, Mrs Manfred,' Nanny was still addicted to the royal 'We'. 'We shan't even have a little headache.'

Kate glared at the two beaming, satisfied faces and her glare became a scowl as she heard Nanny's parting remark, 'We've been such a brave girl, haven't we?' Her scowl turned to an expression of acute dislike and she closed her eyes. She didn't want them, she wanted to talk to Jerome, and now they'd put her to sleep! She could feel the drowsiness stealing over her and she gulped on her sadness.

A hand on her shoulder wakened her and she looked up to see Jerome bending over her with Hattie in the background looking more sour and bad-tempered than ever. But, she congratulated herself, she was feeling much better, the trembling had ceased and she was conscious of an acute hunger. She eyed the tray in Hattie's hands greedily, hoping that there was something substantial on it and that it wasn't sloppy invalid's food.

Jerome caught the look and chuckled, 'We're not starving you, Kate!' and she heard Hattie's outraged snort.

'First time I've ever served steak to an invalid in bed!'

'But I'm not an invalid, Hattie, I'm a heroine,' Kate smiled at the woman, 'and I'm malingering, didn't you know?'

Jerome cut off Hattie's sharp answer with a mild, 'I'll bring the tray down later, don't bother to come up for it,' and when the housekeeper had gone, he made himself comfortable on a chair by the bed and prepared to watch his wife eating.

'You said "explanations".' Kate cut vigorously into a thick steak. 'That was hours ago. How much longer do I have to wait?' She chewed and spoke impolitely through a mouthful of food. 'Do you know what you are? You're an arrogant, impossible man,' she gulped to swallow, 'and what's more,' with an empty mouth, the words came out more clearly, 'you're secretive. Why didn't you tell me you'd destroyed those negatives instead of holding them up for ransom?'

'I wanted the ransom.' He looked darkly goodhumoured. 'I went to a lot of trouble to get you, Kate, and I meant to keep you.' He smiled down at her. 'Do you want the whole story?' and at her nod, he smiled again. 'I started off with the negatives, a missing sister and a mysterious Miss Noelle Lowe who seemed to have no beginnings anywhere. Then at last my enquiry agents turned up with a copy of Kate Forrest's birth certificate, which made things much easier for me. I saw how I could get Philip and Noelle Lowe both at the same time.'

'But you had to find me first.' She pushed aside the empty steak plate and started on a mammoth portion of creamy rice pudding.

'Oh no, I'd already found you.' He chuckled at her gasp of surpise. 'Kate and Philip had vanished; Kate was friendly with a struggling artist called Helen; Helen had a cottage she let out. No difficulty there. It was simply a matter of using a little blackmail, applying just the right amount of force. Don't look like that, my dear. You had a lot of preconceived notions about me, I merely acted up to your idea of the sort of person I was.'

'And Estelle?' she hesitated. Jerome was being nice and she didn't want anything to spoil it.

His face darkened and became withdrawn. 'An area where I miscalculated,' he admitted ruefully. 'I've known her all her life and then she started chasing me in earnest. I kissed her a couple of times, that was all. I'm only human, Kate, and in those days, when something was offered, I took it provided there were no strings attached. I didn't count on her fantasising a couple of kisses into a full-blown affair. To me, she was still part child. No matter what she's said or implied, there was no more to it than that. She's not my type.'

Kate found herself feeling very sorry for Estelle, but she crushed the feeling down. 'What is your type?'

He ticked off on his fingers. 'Five foot eight, slim, red hair, green eyes. You ought to know, Kate. I married her.'

'But you thought I was. . . .' She hesitated, flushing with embarrassment. 'And you only did it to get Philip.'

The withdrawn look had gone from his face and his mouth curved nicely into a smile as he removed the dish from her grasp and set it aside with the tray. 'Anything that had happened before we met didn't matter to me, and I didn't do it just to get Philip.'

'Philip.' Her mouth drooped a little. 'I don't see much of him nowadays, he doesn't seem to need me any more. He's growing away from me.'

'Then you can devote yourself to me.' Jerome sounded very well content with this state of affairs. 'Didn't I mention it in my list of the qualities necessary in a wife? Loving, obedient, faithful, and, of course, devoted!'

'But it's all on one side,' Kate wailed. 'You've never said, never even hinted. So stop looking so damned smug and superior. You know what I mean!'

'Kate!' He leaned forward and let a fingertip caress her mouth, the finger tip slid to her chin, halted there momentarily and then began a tantalising journey down the column of her throat. She reached up and captured it.

'Stop that,' she whispered in a trembling voice. 'We're supposed to be having a serious discussion.'

'And you remember what I told you before about not wanting practical discussions when I'm giving pleasure . . .?'

'Say it, then,' it was a husky murmur. 'Tell me!'

'I tell you every day, every time I touch you. You know I do, and every night as well. I touch you often enough, don't I? I can't keep my hands off you! God, woman, what more do you want? An affidavit?'

'Cavalier!' She inched away from him, holding the marauding finger firmly against her breast. What she was going to say might spoil everything, but she had to say it. 'Shirley,' she mumbled the name half under her breath, and then, 'Theo.'

The grey eyes looking into hers were serious, but there was no pain in them. 'They were very young, I'm trying to remember that, and they were both a bit selfish.' By this time he was sitting on the bed, facing her. 'Not like us, my Kate, we're adult, we can handle it.' He bent his black head, and Kate, fighting the delicious languor which was creeping over her, pushed him away; not very far, though.

'And what are we going to do about Estelle?'

He pulled her back, close to him. 'Forget her!' He dismissed Estelle as though the girl had ceased to exist, but Kate could not be as ruthless.

'She loves you,' there was distress in her voice, 'and I know what it's like, loving you. It's hell!'

His mouth hovered over hers teasingly. 'Hell, Kate?'

Very softly, she sighed as she pulled his head down to hers. 'No, not hell—heaven!'

Harlequin Plus
THE BEAUTY OF CALABRIA

If Italy can be said to be shaped like a great boot kicking out into the Mediterranean, then Calabria is the tip of the toe. Surrounded by the turquoise waters of the Ionian Sea on the east and the Tyrrhenian Sea on the west, the Calabrian coast is said to be a place where the combined beauty of rugged mountains and windswept sea is unrivaled.

Calabria was once considered a harsh land, where a hot sun waxed mercilessly from morning to night. Few travelers made the torturous overland journey through the precipitous mountains to the coast. But today tourists heading for the Calabrian coast enjoy following the Autostrade de Sole—Freeway of the Sun—which leads south from Naples.

On the drive down through the green peaks of the Calabrian Apenines, visitors are entranced by fabulous vistas of the sapphire blue waters of the Tyrrhenian Sea. The autostrada then heads through valleys of citrus, chestnut and fig orchards; past herds of sheep and goats grazing in rocky fields or among the broken ruins of Roman temples. As the road wends its way through sunbaked peasant villages, the silhouettes of great medieval castles and Byzantine churches can be seen in the distance—for Calabria is a place where history was built on top of histroy.

The most recent colonists in Calabria are the result of the growing tourist industry. The ever present sun, which at one time kept people away, now attracts thousands of sunworshippers come to tan and swim on the miles of sand beach wedged between the craggy cliffs and the warm blue Mediterranean waters.

NOW...

8 NEW

Harlequin ◈ *Presents*...

EVERY MONTH!

Romance readers everywhere have expressed their delight with Harlequin Presents, along with their wish for more of these outstanding novels by world-famous romance authors. Harlequin is proud to meet this growing demand with 2 more NEW Presents every month—a total of 8 NEW Harlequin Presents every month!

MORE of the most popular romance fiction in the world!

No one touches the heart of a woman quite like Harlequin.